EVIL EYE

by
Jackie Kaines
and illustrated by Joanna Roberts

HENDERSON
PUBLISHING LTD
©1996 HENDERSON PUBLISHING LTD

For Mum, with love and thanks
for all your help and support

Chapter 1

"They searched the forest, and combed the undergrowth — but the bodies of the children were never found. If you go to the forest on a dark, clear night, you can hear the children's pitiful whimpering, whispering despairingly through the trees."

"Spooky story, Amy!" Kerima was the first of the three listening girls to shake herself back into reality. "Where did you hear it?"

"I made it up!" cried Amy triumphantly, leaping from the sofa with such energy that she sent a cascade of lipsticks, eyeshadows, tweezers and sundry items of clothing to the floor. "What did you think, Beth, Daisy? Pretty scary, huh?"

"Not bad, not bad," grinned Beth, stretching her long, slim legs into the space just made by Amy, until they almost pushed the arm off the already dilapidated sofa. She yawned loudly and rubbed her fingers through her short-cropped blond hair. "You know me, I'd rather have a true story any day."

"Well," said Daisy, shifting her position on a grubby yellow beanbag. "It's your turn next. Amaze us with truth!"

"Yeah," said Amy, her bright blue eyes flashing at Beth. "Let's hear your story."

"Okay." Beth stood up and walked purposefully over to the window. She gazed out into the darkening October sky and jerked the curtains across the window. "Recently," she said, "you've probably read the stories in the papers about the Beast of Lowlake Moor?"

Kerima, Daisy and Amy all made "yes" sounding grunts.

"Well," said Beth, "someone who comes into the Coffee Stop has seen it." Beth worked weekends and some evenings in the local café, and the stories the customers told her were a constant source of amusement to the girls.

"Yeah, yeah." Amy shifted restlessly on the sheet covering a lump that must once have been an armchair. "Big deal!"

"Don't be like that," said Kerima. Beth smiled at her. Amy continued to scowl.

"So who is this person, then?" said Daisy.

"Well, normally I wouldn't pay it any attention." Beth stood in front of the full length mirror on the wall, and hitched her skirt up a couple of inches. "Hmm," she said, "what do you think, should I shorten it?"

"Oh come on Beth!" said Kerima laughing. "Who claims to have seen the dreaded Beast?"

"Well, it was a friend of my Dad who some-times pops into the Coffee Stop in the evenings."

Amy yawned ostentatiously.

"For those who are interested." Beth shrugged as if it did not worry her one way or another. "This guy my Dad knows has a really cute dog. It looks like a greyhound, but it's not. You know, what are they called?"

"A whippet?" suggested Daisy.

"A lurcher," said Amy, pulling faces at herself in a hand mirror.

"Lurcher! That's it," said Beth.

Amy pressed her lips together. "Pink just isn't my colour," she said to her reflection. "Sorry, Beth, your story. What were you saying?"

Beth raised her eyebrows at Amy. "Well, this guy was walking with his dog high on the brow of the moor. It was late — past midnight — and it was teeming with rain. You know how the wind sweeps across the moors and makes the rain slash right into your eyes and face? Well, that's just how it was. Obviously he could barely see. It didn't actually bother him — he walked that route with his dog every night, and they could find their way blindfolded.

"What he saw next," Beth continued, glancing around her as if someone else might be listening, "made him wish he *was* blindfolded. Darkness or no darkness, rain or no rain, there was absolutely no mistaking that the thing heading right towards him was the Beast of Lowlake. His dog started howling. A streak of lightning lit up the wind-ravaged moor." At this point the other three groaned.

"Okay," conceded Beth, "I made that bit up. Anyway, as you can imagine, the poor guy nearly fainted on the spot. He would have run, but his legs didn't want to work anymore. All he could do was stand rooted to the spot, his dog cowering at his ankles, while this gross beast bore down on him. He told me that he felt like throwing up there and then, but the fear made the nausea stick in his throat."

"What did it look like?" Daisy leant forward.

"Did it make a noise?" asked Kerima, fiddling with the tassles on the rug on which she was sprawled. Amy remained silent, reaching behind her armchair to pick at some Blu-Tack which was poking out from the corner of a psychedelic 3-D poster.

"Apparently," said Beth quietly, "it was about three metres high. Its flesh hung off it in great folds, and it was completely hairless. It gave off a sickly-sweet smell, that got into your nostrils and made you gag. It squelched as it moved and made a low weeping noise that echoed in your head. This guy was literally glued to the spot as the huge beast shuffled towards him and his dog, and he was convinced it was going to swamp both of them. It was," Beth paused, closed her eyes and swallowed. "It was...a giant jelly baby!"

"Oh Beth!" giggled Kerima. "You are stupid!"

"Yeah, good one," Daisy grinned.

Even Amy had to smother a smile. The smile was short-lived, however. "Making up stories is all very well," she said. "But what really frightens you? What is the thing that you're most scared of in all the world? I mean like serious fear." Amy tucked her legs under her, rucking up the sheet on the armchair with her heavy black boots as she did so. She glanced at each of the other girls in turn. "Beth?"

"It has to be spiders," said Beth, without hesitation. "I know it's pathetic, but I'm absolutely petrified of them. I don't know what it is. All those legs I suppose. My mum was furious with me the other day. She went to use the vacuum cleaner and I'd taped over the end." The others laughed, waiting for Beth to give them the punchline. "When I went to take a shower, there was one of those giant spiders that lurk in the bathtub. You know the ones? However much water you blast at them they refuse to get sucked down the plughole. Anyway, even if they do go down, you know the wretched things are going to crawl right back out again. Yuk! So — "

"So you used the vacuum to suck it up and then stuck tape over the end to stop it crawling out?" Daisy finished for her.

"You got it!" laughed Beth. She turned to Amy, "I'm laughing now but boy do those creatures bug me!"

Kerima groaned. "Bug you! Very good, Beth. For me it's blood." Daisy nodded in agreement. Kerima spoke energetically, making her dark curls bounce vigorously. "Mind you, I'm not that great with ketchup either!" Everyone laughed. "But blood — it's my worst nightmare. My blood, other people's blood, just keep it away from me! What about you Daisy?"

"I — I..." Daisy blushed.

"Come on Daisy — and it must be the truth!"

Daisy's discomfort seemed to cheer Amy up.

"Just between us, yeah? You won't tell anyone?"

"'Course not!" Kerima spoke encouragingly.

"You know we won't," said Amy. "Just get on with it!"

"Water. I'm really nervous of water."

"But your dad's a swimming instructor!" laughed Beth.

"Oh, thanks for reminding me Beth! I'd forgotten that!" Daisy could have been spitting acid. "Don't you think I get hounded about it every day?"

"I wondered why you were never keen on swimming trips!" Kerima spoke as if she had just discovered the answers to the whole of their GCSE maths paper.

"I don't mind the trips, and the hanging round the edge of the pool watching the talent — 'specially if Pete Hobson's there!" Beth and Kerima laughed with Daisy. Amy tutted disgustedly — boys were clearly out as far as she was concerned. "It's getting into the water I can't stand."

"Do your folks give you a hard time, then?" Beth shook her head disbelievingly.

"Tell me about it!" Daisy sighed. "Anyway, what about you, Amy — what's your phobia?"

"Oh nothing!" said Amy airily. "Nothing scares me that much."

"Out of order, Amy!" cried Beth. "You've had us reveal our inner fears, now it's your turn."

"Oh, what does it matter anyway?" Amy was suddenly angry. "How many years have we known each other? None of this is a surprise, is it? If we're not here at Kerima's, we're in the Coffee Stop, or at Tiger's Disco, or just hanging out. We know each other back to front! Inside out and upside down." She glared at the others. "If Daisy has a spot, we know when it's developing, when it's got a head, and when it's splattered all over the mirror. For heaven's sake! I mean, we need to live, to have some real excitement! Who cares if Beth is frightened of spiders? We all knew she was anyway!" Even the various wall posters seemed to gape open-mouthed as Amy ranted.

"Well," said Kerima placidly, "I didn't know that Daisy was frightened of water. I never knew that." She smiled at Daisy. But Amy was not to be pacified.

"I repeat," she said dramatically, "what does it matter? I mean in the overall scheme of things? Who gives a hoot if poor old Daisy is scared of water!"

Daisy, Beth and Kerima blinked at Amy. They were momentarily too stunned to speak. Sure, the four of them did know each other inside out. Rows with parents and siblings were dissected; clothes were shared; period pains discussed. That was what made life worth living. They had separate lives, yes. Boyfriends and outside interests. But boyfriends came and went. The four had always been there for each other if the going got tough. Through thick and thin, they all stuck together. They had rows, yes, but they got over it.

It had to be said, though, Amy had been really hard work lately. Everything they did was wrong. It was easy just to blame Amy for the increase in petty niggles between them. But the nagging doubt hung in the air around them. Did they really like each other, or was this friendship just a childhood habit that was hard to kick? Was Amy simply being more honest than the rest of them? Were they hanging on to something that just wasn't there anymore?

Daisy and Kerima were desperately trying to ride the storm in the hope that Amy would settle down again, restore the balance. Beth was less diplomatic.

"Sor-ree," she said belligerently. "If we're not dramatic enough for you, perhaps you'd better get out there and really live! Rob a bank, maybe? Drop out of school completely…you're hardly there these days anyway."

Amy dragged herself out of the armchair. She glared angrily at Beth.

"I might just do that!" she hissed. "At least it's better than sitting round here, telling babyish stories and exchanging pointless gossip. We might all be dead tomorrow." Her eyes flashed angrily. "I for one am going to get a life before that happens — get some excitement!" She grabbed her overnight bag, and marched towards the door.

10

As she opened the door, Beth spoke. "Say, Amy, want a piece of advice?" Amy flashed a look of pure disgust at Beth. Undeterred, Beth continued, "Whatever you do, change the lippy. You were right, pink just isn't your colour!"

The force of the door slamming behind Amy rocked the whole of Kerima's house.

Beth, Amy and Kerima heard a mumbled exchange between Amy and Kerima's mum. Kerima smiled anxiously. She didn't expect Amy to go overboard thanking Mum for her hospitality and all that, but she hoped Amy was not downright rude.

They all heard the front door shut. It was impossible to judge anything from the way it shut — at least it wasn't slammed.

"I just don't get her!" exclaimed Beth, jumping up and peering out of the window. She watched Amy's compact figure stride out of view. "She wanted to tell horror stories — which let's face it, we all felt was a smidgen childish, but we went ahead anyway. She wanted to know our deepest fears — which was a little tedious, but we all confessed. She gets everything she wants and still she's not happy."

"She's not interested in anything anymore. Did you see her at Tiger's last night? She just sat in the corner glaring at everyone, like they hadn't had her permission to exist, let alone have a good time!" Daisy sucked in her cheeks.

The others nodded. "Say," said Beth, "talking of Tiger's, Kerima, looked like you were giving

Danny King some serious mouth-to-mouth resuscitation."

"Yes," said Daisy, "you were spotted, Kerima. Is this something you wish to share with us?"

Kerima pulled a face at them. "I think I can safely say I have no comment. Let's move on shall we?"

Daisy laughed. Then she glanced at her watch. "Message received and understood. I'm going to have to get home pretty soon, guys. You know we've got that school trip tomorrow?"

"What, to the local museum?" said Beth. "Big deal!"

"You're beginning to sound like Amy," said Daisy. "I think it sounds quite interesting — I'd like to see some of the stuff they got from that archaeological dig on the edge of the moors. Apparently they've found some stuff that's really well-preserved."

"Maybe they found a jelly print!" said Kerima. "What I love is wandering through the Mystic Room," she continued. "You know Stonybrook Museum has one of the biggest collection of ancient, mystic artefacts from around the world, in this country?" She directed the question at Beth.

"I didn't know that," admitted Beth. "In fact, I've never been to the museum."

"Never been!" The other two tutted in mock shock.

Beth grinned. "Well, I vaguely remember the parentals forcing me to go when I was knee high to a grasshopper."

"Well, there's a first time for everything," said Daisy. "Besides, anything's better than double science! I'm off, I'll see you two tomorrow." She stopped with her hand on the doorknob. "Oh blast! I almost forgot, I promised to drop by and see Ashleigh." She glanced at her watch. "I might just have time. Nine o'clock curfew on a Sunday!" The others laughed.

"How is Ashleigh? She doesn't do many of the same classes as me," said Beth.

Ashleigh had moved to Stonybrook and joined the High School the last term of year 10. She was slightly zany and rebellious, which fitted well with them. She worked reasonably hard at school, but her life did not revolve around GCSEs and achieving the perfect grade for homework assignments. Daisy and she lived in the same street and saw a lot of each other.

"She's fine," said Daisy.

"Why doesn't she hang out more with the rest of us?" asked Kerima. "We could do with some new blood."

"Thought you said you hated blood!" Beth and Daisy chorused. They all laughed.

"Right," said Daisy. "The fact is, she finds Amy hard work. She thinks Amy's dangerous. And, the way she was tonight, I'm beginning to think she could be right. Anyway, I'm really going now. See ya!"

"See you, Daisy!" Beth and Kerima chorused

as Daisy clumped off down the stairs.

Kerima picked up a couple of empty drink cans and threw them at the bin. She scored one hit — and one miss. She groaned. Beth sat down on the edge of the armchair, silently watching as Kerima bent to mop up the sticky dregs of drink now splattered up the bin, the walls and across the floor. Kerima was so lucky having this room all to herself, like a private sitting room. And her parents were really laid back. If Beth invited even one person to sleep over, her mum would be fussing about bedding and food and everything else a week beforehand. Kerima would just turn up home and say: "Hi Mum. Hi Dad. Amy, Beth and Daisy are staying the night. See you tomorrow." They'd all troop upstairs and that would be that. That was how people their age should be treated.

"Do you think I was mean to Amy?" Beth said.

Kerima stood up and shrugged. "It's difficult when she's like that. I mean we all understand, but..."

"We do?" said Beth.

"I think it's still her cousin."

"Ah," said Beth, blushing slightly. "I hadn't exactly forgotten, but it's a year ago now — I just thought she'd have settled down. Mind you, I s'pose you never get over something like that."

"If anything, it's worse now than ever." Kerima's dark eyebrows swept together above worried eyes. "When Ben died in that fire, she was stunned. I mean, you remember, she just walked around in a daze."

Beth nodded. "Yeah. Poor girl. Then she cried for weeks — do you remember? When that stopped, I guess I thought she'd come to terms with it. Or maybe I just hoped she had."

"I thought so too at first. But you know she's always been a bit wilder than the rest of us. And it's like, unless she makes something dramatic happen, she's just not going to be happy. I wish she'd talk about it. But she just says there's nothing wrong. She says she doesn't think about Ben and the fire. She's just bored." Kerima sighed. "You know, Beth, maybe Ashleigh is right. Perhaps Amy's going to do something stupid soon — something dangerous. And there's absolutely nothing we can do about it."

Whilst Kerima and Beth were discussing her welfare, Amy had arrived home. In answer to her dad's question about joining him for supper she had muttered, "Not hungry".

Upstairs in her bedroom, she flicked on some music, cranking up the volume to just above what she knew to be an acceptable level. Sure enough her dad's voice rose above the beat of the music.

"Down, Amy!"

Amy sighed and flicked the switch. She felt so restless. Since Ben had died she had been haunted by images of his death. He'd been at an illegal party — one step on from a rave — and the warehouse where it was being held had caught fire. There'd been lots of terrible injuries.

But only one death — Amy's cousin, Ben. Of course the effect on their family had been catastrophic. But, although that was difficult, it was not what really worried Amy. What really got to her was the fact that she knew she could have saved Ben's life.

She sat on the edge of her bed, rocking backwards and forwards, her head in her hands.

"It's my fault he died," she moaned to herself for the millionth time. "My fault. I could have saved him. I should have saved him!"

She leapt to her feet, pacing up and down her small bedroom. She was going to have to do something. That was the only way to get these thoughts out of her head. She gazed at her school books on her desk, exactly where she had left them on Friday evening. The violent urge to sweep them off was too much. Pens, pencils, ornaments all clattered to the floor.

Since nothing happens in this awful place, I'm just going to have to make it happen! And soon, thought Amy wildly.

Chapter 2

Fire. Searing, blinding fire. It was all around her, leaping up out of the ground like an iridescent oil slick. Through the flames, a face appeared. A face, plastic-white against smoke-black streaks. She knew who it was without having to look. But it was impossible not to look at the begging eyes. His lips were moving. She bent through the heat of the flames to try and catch his words.

The roar of the flames, like one hundred thundering waterfalls, made it impossible to hear. But she could read his lips all right.

"Save me," he mouthed at her. "Save me!" Her hands flew to her ears. She tried to shut her eyes. But the lips kept moving, "Save me!"

A piercing scream woke Amy. She was bolt upright in bed. Her hair was glued to her face with sweat, her T-shirt clung in wet bubbles to her body. Her mouth was wide open. It was her. She was screaming, screaming, screaming...

Her bedroom door burst open.

"Amy! Oh Amy!" Her dad rushed to her bed, thumping down beside her. She was rigid in his arms, still screaming. "Hush, now. It's okay. It's okay. It was a dream, love. Just a dream."

At last Amy was quiet. She subsided into her dad's arms, sobbing. She did not know how long he sat there, stroking her hair. Her mind was numb. If Dad knew, if he knew what she had done or, rather, what she had not done. He would not be comforting her. He would hate her. They would all hate her.

"Just a dream, love." His voice was like a long-lost echo coming back to haunt her.

She pushed his arms away. He looked at her, startled. Before he could say anything, Amy shoved him again in the chest.

"Oh, no," she said slowly. "No, Dad, it's not a dream. It's a nightmare."

"Beth and Amy were at it like two sumo wrestlers last night," said Daisy, pulling a leaf off one of the rowan trees that stood like sentries guarding the pavement. Ashleigh gave a shrug, a 'so what's new?' shrug. She glanced behind her.

"Hurry up, Toby," she yelled. Her little brother was a few metres behind them, poking with his toe-cap at what was left of a dead pigeon. "Come on, you little mutant! Leave it." She turned to Daisy. "Isn't he gross? Toby! If I have to come and get you, I'll pull your ears, stamp on your toes and rub your nose in that apology for a bird!"

"You couldn't catch me!" Toby left his gruesome task and ambled towards them.

"Sad boy!" Daisy laughed as she spoke.

"Most sad," agreed Ashleigh.

At that moment a loud whoop made them

forget Toby. Beth was dancing towards them, arms and legs waving.

"I think Beth's been busy with the sewing machine," said Daisy. "Her clothes are amazing!" Beth stood in front of them, panting from the exertion of her outrageous dance down the street. "So, you went for shortening the skirt, then?"

"Oh yes!" She shook a skinny leg at them. "What d'you think?"

"Nearly as short as your hair," said Ashleigh.

"You're just jealous."

"Something like that." Ashleigh glanced down at her own jeans. She couldn't wear the kind of extravagant clothes that Beth designed, not in a million years. She'd look stupid.

The group turned into the school gates, joining the stream of kids heading for the day's torture.

"Those earrings should be had up by the child protection agency," said Daisy. "Your neck'll be black and blue at the end of the day! Where did you get them?"

"I made them. I thought they were suitably ancient-looking for the trip to the Mu-zee-um."

They waved Toby into the junior block. "Say," said Ashleigh, "there's Amy. Boy, she looks even more cheerful than usual — not!"

Amy was slouching against the pillar by the senior block entrance. She was hunched into a black bomber jacket. Her dark hair was swept back from her face. Her eyes were dark, haunted caverns in a pinched, white face.

"Talk about Mrs Death!" muttered Beth. Daisy glared at her.

"You're not exactly normal to look at."

"Meow!" said Ashleigh, then, "Hi Amy!"

Amy acknowledged the greeting with a grunt.

"I thought maybe you wouldn't be here today. That you'd be out really living!"

Amy narrowed her eyes at Beth, then she grinned. "Yeah, well, I couldn't miss the treat of the year, now could I? Besides, I've got an idea that this museum trip might be more *lively* than we expect." Amy turned on her heel and strode into school. Beth pulled a face, and Daisy and Ashleigh shrugged.

"It sounds like we might be in for an interesting visit, then?" said Ashleigh.

Before the others could say anything, Kerima wafted past, eyeball to eyeball with Danny King.

"Get that!" hissed Beth as Danny and Kerima headed along the corridor.

"That girl has got some detailed confessions to make!" said Daisy.

It may have been pleasantly cool and autumnal outside, but in the museum it was hot and dry from the central heating. The curator's voice droned on like a bee giving a whole bunch of flowers serious grief.

Kerima's eyelids drooped. Daisy yawned and Beth fidgeted.

"Thought you said this would be interesting,"

she hissed in Daisy's ear. Daisy grimaced.

"I didn't expect a blow-by-blow account of every clod of earth lifted to find the wretched stuff! Anyway, I told you, it's the Mystic Room that's really cool. There are some great stories..."

"Ahem." Mr Bolton's cough was his most effective weapon of discipline. Beth glared at him, and he glared right back. She tried to listen again.

"So," the man was saying, "we thought at first that this was purely a Roman site, which fits in with other finds in the area. But then we began to realise that some of the artefacts we had unearthed pre-dated that time." He paused for effect. But it took a lot more than a dramatic pause to impress year 11 from Stonybrook High. The guy blushed slightly, then ploughed on. "Yes, it soon became clear that we were looking at..." He isn't bad-looking, mused Beth. Shame he's so deadly dull.

She scanned the room to see what the rest of the class was up to.

Just behind her, something caught her eye. She was sure she glimpsed someone disappearing through one of the exits. Who was leaving the room? She was pretty sure she knew who it was. Another glance around the room confirmed that Amy was not there. So, what was she up to?

Beth decided she might just as well find out. Anything to get out of this room. Bolton was well engrossed. Gently she edged backwards. In the space of a minute, she too slid from the room.

She found herself in a large, airy gallery. It made the room she'd just left seem like a broom cupboard. This was what you imagined real museums to look like. Pillars, showcases with small exhibits, and, more impressively, large exhibits cordoned off with red or blue rope. Some of the exhibits were breathtaking.

The figure in front of her quite clearly came from Africa. Wood, planed so smooth it looked like soap, swept up to create the neck of the statue. Out of its face broke a nose, round bulbous eyes and a tongue that stretched past its chin. As she took in the rest of the room, Beth realised she was in the Mystic Gallery that Daisy and Kerima had spoken about. She glanced behind her. There was something creepy about being in here with no one else around. Where had Amy disappeared to? Perhaps she'd gone to the loo?

A fantastic figure caught her eye. It took pride of place in the centre of the room. She moved towards it. She was drawn not just by its magnificence, but she felt also a curious urge to be closer to it...

She stood in front of the weird figure, staring at it eye to eye. The eyes were made from some kind of jewel that glowed black and purple. They were set in the carved face of what looked like a cross between a mystical beast and a devil. The creature's body was that of a human — but a human with both male and female sex organs. Beth gazed into the eyes and felt a surge of panic rise inside her. She shook her head and studied the caption of the statue in an attempt to dispel the feeling.

"INSTATA. This South American tribe was renowned for its intricate carvings of both practical and ornamental goods. They were particularly keen on creating powerful icons like GRANTA, seen here. Granta was the Instata's foremost and most widely worshipped god. They believed it to be keeper of all human fears. The Instata worshipped the icon in the hope that it would relieve them of their fears. Legend has it that the Instata, whose use of magic and witchcraft is well-documented, invested their icons with magical forces that could be unleashed in the form of curses and bad luck on those who dared meddle with their gods' powers. There are a number of deaths and incidents that have been linked to the Instata's magic, but nothing that has conclusively proven the veracity of the legend."

Beth looked at Granta. It felt like Granta was looking right back at her with those dark, unfathomable eyes. Well, Beth thought, magic or no magic, legend or no legend, she did not fancy messing with Granta, keeper of fear. She was just deciding whether she could safely turn her back on the statue, when a voice made the decision for her.

"And what do you think you're doing?"

Beth spun round to face Amy.

"You nearly frightened the life out of me!

Where have you been? What are you up to?"

"That talk was enough to stifle the life out of me." Amy laughed. "Pretty impressive, huh?" She nodded at Granta. "Those eyes are like the Mona Lisa's, they seem to follow you everywhere." She paused. "Fear! Who was it who said 'the only thing we have to fear is fear itself?' Who cares about fear!" Amy spat the words out as if they tasted dirty.

"What on earth are you going on about?" Beth frowned. "More to the point, what exactly have you been up to?"

"I went to the loo and decided these things were a fraction more interesting than bits of dirty Roman bone found on the moor."

"This place is pretty creepy, though."

"I like it."

"Yeah, me too, but when I was here on my own, well..."

"You weren't alone."

"Were you hiding? Watching me? I thought you might be!"

"No. Granta was with you!" Amy waved her arms dramatically.

The door creaked open and Beth's laugh died in her throat. Bolton!

"What on earth are you two up to?"

"Amy felt faint, Sir. It's really stuffy in that room. I brought her out to get some air. We were just on our way to the loo, for her to splash her face with cold water, Sir."

Bolton glared at them. "Get a move on then."

Back in the lecture room, the curator finally exhausted his supply of information. Questions were a short affair, since no one could even be bothered to make the effort to ask one, not even out of politeness.

They were just about to leave when a man in a dark suit entered the room and spoke to the curator.

"Ooh lovely," muttered Daisy, "they've decided to give us an extra lecture." The others all grinned.

One of the boys said, "Look, there's a couple of cops outside." Sure enough, two blue uniformed figures lurked outside the door.

"Looks like they've come to arrest you and Danny King for indecent behaviour." Amy nudged Kerima. Kerima scrunched up her face and pushed her hair back from her forehead.

"Jealousy, my dear, will get you nowhere!"

Bolton joined the two men. They huddled together. "Looks grim," said Kerima. "I wonder what's going on."

The suited man left the room and started talking to the police. Bolton turned to address the class.

"Right." He shifted uncomfortably. "Unfortunately there has been a crime committed in the museum while we've been here." Some bright spark went "wooo-oooo". Bolton glared. "The police wish to speak to the whole class. They're particularly keen to speak to Amy and Beth."

Beth's stomach lurched. Hot and cold

prickles scratched at her face and neck. She glared at Amy. Amy grinned and shrugged. "Well, come on you two." Bolton's worry came out as irritation.

"I...You want us to come now, Sir?" Beth hated the stutter that crept into her voice. Amy leapt to her feet and bowed ostentatiously to the rest of the class. Several people giggled.

"Come on, Watson, we can crack this case!" she said to Beth.

"This is serious, you two," Bolton murmured to them when they reached him. "You're both under suspicion. Just tell the truth and hopefully we can all be out of here." Beth wanted to ask what the problem was, but there wasn't time.

The girls were shown out to an empty office. Two policewomen eyed them as they entered. One of them, a large woman who towered above her colleague, stood up.

"Right," she said, "Amy, Beth, first of all, I'm going to ask you to let us search your belongings."

Chapter 3

Pulsing, multi-coloured lights licked like flames in the shadowy gloom which encompassed Tiger's Disco. Kerima and Daisy sat at a table watching the stomping figures on the dance floor. They'd both just been dancing, and Kerima's dark curls clung damply to her forehead, whilst Daisy's chest still heaved from the exertion.

Daisy touched Kerima's arm and pointed to the far side of the floor. Amy stood just to the left of the entrance, caught in a halo of glowing light. She was peering round the room. Finally she spotted them and, with a wave, she pressed her way through the mass of people. Slamming a bottle of mineral water on to the table, Amy sat down. She kicked her trademark black DMs onto a spare chair.

"Yo!" she yelled above the heavy beat of the music. "Where's Beth?" Amy had to repeat her question before the other two heard her.

"She had to work." Kerima leant right forward, her lips nearly touching Amy's ear. "She'll see us at mine later. Are you staying?"

"Sure. Hey, I love this one, I'm going to dance." So saying, Amy took a swig of water and leapt to her feet. Several people acknowledged her presence on the floor with salutes and nods.

Daisy moved closer to Kerima, "She's

cheered up!"

Kerima nodded her agreement, "Seems she enjoyed Monday's case of the missing eye. I just hope this lasts."

They watched Amy bouncing on the dance floor. Suddenly she stopped. She lurched into a couple dancing beside her. Falling bodies were not unusual at Tiger's, and they shoved her out of the way.

"What's she up to?" yelled Daisy. At that moment, Amy fell to her knees, clutching her head. People near her paused in their dancing and stared. One guy bent down and touched her shoulder. Kerima was already on her feet rushing towards Amy. As she reached her, Amy struggled to her feet, pushing aside the guy's helping hand. He shrugged and started dancing again.

Amy let herself be led from the floor by Kerima. Kerima took her to the toilets, but, as usual, they were heaving with people sitting on sinks, on toilet seats and on the floor. Boys and girls generally hanging out - chatting, a few of them smoking, and several couples in tight clinches. Great atmosphere, but not if you've just collapsed on the dance floor.

"Shall we get back to my place?" Kerima asked Amy. Amy's pale face was damp with sweat.

"Yeah," she said, "let's." Then, as an afterthought, "D'you mind? What about DK?"

"All off!" said Kerima. "Anyway, it's nearly 11.00, I've just about had it."

"We're out of here then!" said Amy.

In the cold night air Kerima and Amy jiggled up and down as Daisy struggled into her coat.

"What happened back there then?" said Daisy as they moved off along the pavement.

Amy shrugged. "Dunno. Nothing really. Combination of the lights and stuff…" She faltered. The image of flames licking up her legs and across her bare arms sent a renewed wave of fear and pain rushing through her. She gritted her teeth. This was crazy! Her imagination was running away with her. Well, she wouldn't let it anymore. She was going to have fun! "C'mon," she yelled, "I'm fine now!"

Daisy and Kerima looked at each other. "Weird!" said Daisy.

The warmth of Kerima's parents' central heating was sheer bliss after the crisp coolness of the night and Daisy, Kerima and Amy settled down in Kerima's sitting room with coffee and several packets of biscuits.

"Are you all right now?" Daisy tried again.

Amy looked surprised. "Sure! Why shouldn't I be?"

"Come off it, Amy, you collapsed on the dance floor! What happened?"

"Nothing. I just got dizzy, that's all. Stop fussing!" She grabbed a chocolate biscuit and munched ravenously at it. She grinned at the other two, with genuine delight, and tried to make up an excuse. "Of course! I haven't really eaten today! Don't you get woozy when you don't eat?"

"I've never not eaten for long enough to find out!" Daisy rubbed her stomach ruefully. "As you may notice!"

"Never! Not!" Kerima shook her head. "I despair of you Daisy! Don't you listen in your English lessons — double negatives are the greatest sin!"

The relief flooded through Amy. It made sense. Everything was ten times worse when you didn't eat. That must have been why she had felt so ill. She grabbed a handful of biscuits and proceeded to shovel them into her mouth and tuned back into the banter between the others.

"*The* worst sin?" Daisy raised a suggestive eyebrow.

"In grammar it is!" Kerima grinned. "It is good to be able to come back here — you know, just us lot." Kerima picked up a biscuit and, without too much lip-stretching, popped it in whole. "Imagine if DK or one of the other boys were here — we wouldn't be able to relax!"

"Ah! Danny King! Are you ready to talk?" Daisy stood with her bottom pressed to a radiator.

"Nothing to say really," said Kerima. "Except imagine this biscuit was that slimy creep!" She snapped a gingernut clean in two.

"We get the picture!" said Daisy. "Oh Kerima, I'm sorry. You really liked him, didn't you?"

Before Kerima could answer, Amy, who had begun to pace restlessly, spoke. "What time d'you reckon Beth'll be here?"

"Any minute." Kerima glanced at her watch.

She raised an eyebrow at Daisy. "I tell you something, Beth's dead uptight about the museum."

"Oh — Beth should lighten up," said Amy, slouching back into the sofa. "She thinks she's so cool in her far-out clothes, working in the Coffee Stop, flirting with all the old fogies. A brief encounter with our friends from the local police force, and she's wetting herself!"

"I'm not sure that's fair," Kerima looked at Daisy.

"As I understand it," said Daisy, "what really ticked her off was this guy you saw."

"Is it my fault if I saw the probable criminal?" Amy held her hands out.

"Beth swears blind there wasn't anyone. She says she would have seen them. She says you're making it up."

"Oh well, it's just a shame that the security cameras weren't working, otherwise I'd prove it to her. Besides, the police believed me."

Beth's voice startled them all.

"So, how come they were in the Coffee Stop asking me questions about your story tonight, then?"

Amy nearly dropped her coffee at the sound of Beth's voice.

"Beth!" said Kerima. "We didn't hear you."

"No — I'd never have guessed," said Beth, shutting the door. "Rule number one, if you're going to have a good old go about someone, make sure the door's shut properly, or, that you've rigged up an early warning system!"

"Were the police really asking more questions?" Amy seemed delighted at the prospect.

"You're warped!" said Beth. "You go round with a face like death and then the first hint of trouble and suddenly the world's all right with you!"

"Oh pack it in you two." Daisy bit into a chocolate biscuit. "What did the police want?"

"Well, apparently, this guy you saw — ho, ho, ho — " Beth grimaced at Amy, "is their only lead. They can't understand how come I didn't see him since we left the lecture room together — and stayed together the whole time." Beth paused. Then she turned to Amy once more, her eyes flashing. "You really dumped me in it!"

"Temper, temper." Amy stood up. "I thought you liked real-life drama. Besides, if you hadn't been so quick to tell Bolton we'd left the room together, we wouldn't be in this mess. As it goes, I saw the guy before you came out."

"But the eye was still there when I was looking at Granta!" yelled Beth. "If the guy had been in, nicked the eye and then disappeared again, the eye wouldn't have been there, would it? Come on, Amy, what do you take me for — a complete idiot? What are you hiding? Do you know who took the eye?"

"No, I don't take you for a complete idiot. Maybe the bloke came back after we went back to that riotous talk. How should I know?

Anyway, I'm sure we'll all be impressed by what you told the police. So, why not tell us."

"I don't believe you..." Beth moved towards Amy; she looked as if she might slap her.

"Come on, Beth," Kerima took Beth's arm. "Take your jacket off and tell us about it."

"Yeah!" said Daisy. "I bet you freaked out when the police walked in at work."

"Well," said Beth, managing a smile at last, "I don't think it did my image too much good! Old smelly Paulo kept rushing over every time I went to the till to ring up. Everyone obviously thought they were being served by a criminal. And Ricky Small and his gang were in, and, as you know, they *are* criminals. So they all think I'm one of them now."

"So," Amy said. "What did you say?"

"Do I detect a bit of anxiety in Amy 'I'm so cool in a crisis'?" Beth paused but Amy did not rise to the bait. "This whole business has really caused a stink. Apparently wretched Granta is on loan to this country from the Brazilian National Museum. It's supposed to be touring key museums in the UK. Now all sorts of you know what has hit the fan. Anyway, I said to the police that when we first came out, I dropped an earring and had to scrabble about looking for it, so that was probably when you saw the bloke."

"There, it wasn't difficult now was it?"

"I don't understand why the security was so lax," Daisy said. "I mean, if this is a Brazilian national treasure, it seems crazy that..."

"It was a series of unlucky coincidences, according to the police."

"I thought the police were questioning you! Seems like they were reporting in to you!" said Kerima. "It wasn't PC Bright by any chance, was it?" After their initial questioning all the girls had agreed that it would be worth getting into trouble to be grilled by PC Bright. The guys had been less impressed with the good PC's charms.

"Him and that woman copper," said Beth grinning. "They were quite nice actually. I don't think they really suspect us — " she turned to Amy, "well, not me, anyway."

"Good, I hope they do suspect me!" said Amy. "Anyway, I don't know what all the fuss is about. The police have got an interesting investigation to carry out, people have got something to be shocked and horrified about, and the museum will make a small fortune out of it!"

"Sometimes," said Beth, narrowing her eyes at Amy, "you are incredibly childish."

"Well," Daisy said quickly, "you guys read that caption. I wouldn't want to be the one to test the legend out! Maybe it's a devil-worshipper?"

"Exactly!" said Beth. "It's got to be someone who's completely barmy, someone who can't read, or someone who's evil!"

"Or," said Amy getting to her feet and

sauntering towards the table with the chocolate biscuits, "someone who just doesn't care!" So saying, she banged her hand on the table.

Daisy, Beth and Kerima gaped at the object on the table in stunned silence.

The silence stretched on. Amy stood facing the other three, her cheeks flushed and a defiant smile twisting at her lips.

When they did finally speak, they all talked at once.

"Oh my..."

"But why did...?"

"I didn't want to believe..."

"That I have no fear?" Amy said.

"Who are you trying to kid?" said Beth. "It's so obvious that you're completely messed up by something — what is it, Amy? Is it your cousin?"

"Steady on, Beth," said Daisy, and Kerima hissed at Beth's words. Amy seemed completely unmoved by Beth's outburst, caught in the glow of her own daring.

"Steady on? Steady on?" Beth paced up and down the small room. "What on earth do you mean? Amy steals the eye out of some ancient mystic icon. Not only has she just got Stonybrook Police Force breathing down our necks, but the international crime squad too, and we're all supposed to sit round and slap her on the back! I don't believe you guys! I just don't believe it!"

"What is it?" Amy's voice was low. "Are you frightened of what might happen? Are you frightened of the evil eye?"

"I don't give a hoot about the wretched eye. I do give a hoot about having the police come and hassle me at work and winding my mum and dad up. I get enough grief from them without them believing I've been involved in some pointless, pathetic crime!"

Amy laughed. "Now who's being a smidgen childish! Who will ever know that we have the eye? Nobody!"

Kerima shrugged. "Amy's right. Who's ever going to guess it was us?"

"But what's the point?" demanded Beth. "What's the blessed point?"

Daisy had moved towards the eye which glowed darkly on the table.

"Wow!" she spoke almost to herself. "Would you just look at that! I mean it's just a jewel of some sort, but it really looks like an eye!"

"Isn't it amazing?" said Amy. "It's like it's actually looking straight through you."

Kerima moved closer to the table and stared down at the purple-black eye. "How does it feel, you know, to touch it?" she said to Amy. "It looks like it would feel like an eye — d'you remember those bulls' eyes we dissected?"

"Touch it and see!" said Amy. "Go on Kerima — it feels really weird, like it's alive."

Very slowly Kerima reached out. Her hand shook slightly as she went to pick up the eye. She picked it up between her thumb and forefinger and held it up to the light. "Granta's eye," she whispered.

Held up like that, the jewel appeared almost like living liquid encased in a fine membrane. Daisy peered up at it.

"Go on, Daisy, feel it," urged Amy.

"For crying out loud!" said Beth. "You sound like some wicked witch under the evil eye's influence already. 'Go on, feel it,'" Beth mimicked.

"We're all in this together," said Amy. "You in particular — considering the lies you've told!"

"I don't believe this!" said Beth. "You've gone completely mad. Are you sure you're all right?"

"You did come over funny at the disco," Kerima carried on staring at the eye. Then very gently, she put it back down. "Maybe the legend is beginning to work!" she turned slowly and dramatically. "Maybe Amy will suffer with migraines for the rest of her life as punishment for meddling with the mighty Granta!" Amy and Daisy giggled. Beth continued to look furious.

"Well!" she said. "Maybe! Who knows what hidden powers these things have? Don't you remember the legend of the pharaoh's curse? Tutankhamen, Lord Carnarvon and all that?"

"This is different!" cried Daisy.

"Why? Why is it different? Wasn't anyone who broke the seal on the tomb s'posed to die? And didn't Carnarvon peg it just afterwards? The Instata were known for their magical spells and powers — who knows what could happen to someone who ripped the eye out of one of their prized gods? Who knows!"

"Have you been taking lessons from the curator or something? For someone who hadn't even been to the museum until a few days ago, you're an amazing expert, Beth!" Kerima obviously found the whole thing a great joke. "Besides — didn't Carnarvon die from an insect bite?"

"Yes! But what made the insect bite him?" The other three hooted with laughter. A smile twitched at the corners of Beth's mouth. "Oh, you know what I mean! Were you really ill at Tiger's?"

Amy was still laughing. "I was just messing about. Setting the scene for this evening's revelation!"

"I thought you were hungry?" said Kerima.

"Well, that too." Amy shrugged. "I felt a bit faint and decided to dramatise it a bit — you know all about dramatisation, Beth!"

"Yeah, yeah!" Beth moved towards Amy. "Well, we all know how reliable you are when it comes to telling the truth — you know, ever heard of honesty, Amy?"

"Oh for heaven's sake, Beth. Why should Amy lie about feeling ill?" Daisy turned on her. "Don't you think you're over-reacting? I mean, look at this eye, it's amazing."

"I don't believe what I'm hearing here! The eye may be amazing, but it also belongs to an ancient Instata god who was supposed to be keeper of human fears..."

At that moment, Amy gasped and fell to her

knees, clasping her head and groaning.

"It's what happened at Tiger's!" said Kerima.

"Amy! Oh my..."

"Oh for heaven's sake, get up Amy! You're so obvious!" Beth walked over to the sofa and kicked her shoes off. "I'm absolutely done in, what with the cops and the post-pub rush at the café tonight. Paulo had to be really vicious to the customers to have his key in the lock by 11.30, which means he gave us a hard time too!"

Daisy and Kerima gawped at Beth, dumbfounded by her apparent callousness.

Amy glanced up from her kneeling position. "Thanks a lot for ruining my performance — all those years at acting classes, for nothing!"

"Oh Amy, give it a rest for heaven's sake!" It was unusual for Kerima to sound so angry. "You've made your point!"

"Your jokes do tend to wear thin, Amy," said Beth. "Anyway, now we've been lumbered with this wretched eye, I suggest we decide what to do with it." Beth glanced fleetingly at the strange gem on the table.

Daisy peered at the eye. She reached out as if to touch it. Her hand hovered over it for the briefest moment, and then, sighing, she picked it up, turning it over between her fingers. "Weird!" she said. "It's like you could drown in it."

"Thought you didn't like water!" Amy and Kerima chorused.

Daisy put the stone down. "Beth is right, though. We need to decide what to do with the eye, now we've got it. Perhaps we should just dump it in a lake or something?"

"That would be terrible," said Kerima. "One of us should keep it until we decide what to do. I don't think it should be Amy — you know, just in case."

"Just in case what?" said Beth.

"Oh, I don't know."

"Well, don't look at me! I'm not going to look after the wretched thing." Beth folded her arms.

"I'll take it," said Daisy. "I don't mind."

"Of course, we could just put it back," said Amy.

The others looked at her. Beth shook her head. "I don't get it...the thrill's over for you now, is it?"

"No, I just thought I'd contribute to the debate."

"If we try and put it back, we'd be bound to be caught," said Kerima. "You know how it is — d'you remember when we agreed to steal those chews from the sweet shop? I felt so guilty I went to put mine back — the woman in the shop caught me and accused me of stealing! I ask you! Me, stealing!"

"Thank you for sharing that with the group Kerima. Just because we were all about eight at the time is neither here nor there. It's very courageous of you to bare your soul! Oh and since we're 'fessing up, you might like to know Kerima, that the rest of us just pretended to steal the chews," said Beth.

"You mean you never actually stole them? I got into all that trouble for nothing? You lot tricked me and you never owned up!"

"We're owning up now Kerima!" Daisy laughed. "Anyway, back to the eye. Let's just hang on to it and dump it when things have quietened down. Like I said, I'll look after it." Daisy looked at the glowing stone again. "Have you noticed how it seems to change colour? When Amy put it down, it was kind of orangey-red. When I touched it, it went a sort of blue colour."

"Yeah!" said Kerima. "When I held it and looked into it, it glowed kind of blood red at its heart!" she stopped. "Creepy!"

"You haven't felt it yet, Beth," said Amy.

"No, and I'm not about to." Beth tucked her hands under her legs.

"Are you scared?" Amy was laughing.

"No, I'm not scared, but I thought I made it clear that I'm not interested in meddling."

"Oh come on!" said Daisy. "If you touch it, we can see if it does change colour."

"Listen you guys, this isn't some kind of pathetic multi-coloured crystal! It's the eye from a god worshipped by a tribe of voodoo practising Indians, hundreds of years ago!"

"Just touch it and shut up!" said Amy.

Beth moved over to the table. She stood and looked down at the eye. Everything seemed to recede. The fidgeting of her friends became a distant hollow echo, before finally disappearing altogether. All Beth could hear was Amy's voice inside her head saying "the only thing we have to fear is fear itself."

Then everything faded away completely. Everything except her consciousness of the eye and of her hand reaching out towards it. The eye glowed browny-black at her. She felt it was challenging her. Not goading her as Amy had done. Finally her fingers brushed the eye.

The minute she saw the creature, Beth snatched her hand away in fear and loathing. Reality fell into place around her. "Where on earth did that foul thing suddenly spring from?" she exclaimed.

The other three looked puzzled.

"That spider — it suddenly shot out from behind the eye. Didn't you see it?"

"Good one Beth!" said Daisy at last. "First you go into a trance, then you see spiders! You're a fine one to talk about Amy!"

"But I saw it: it was there." Beth stared at the eye. It gazed back at her impassively. She looked down at her fingertips, as if they would be marked where she had touched the eye. "I saw a spider — not a big one. But it was a spider. It crawled out from under the eye."

"Look, let's call it a night," said Kerima. "We'll all be seeing things…"

"I did not imagine it!"

"Oh, let's just go to bed!" Kerima began to pull bedding out of cupboards and tossed it haphazardly across the room.

Each girl sank into her own sleeping bag.

As Beth dropped off to sleep the image of the eye burnt into her mind. It cracked open and hundreds of tiny spiders scuttled out. She opened her eyes to dispel the image and glanced around the silent room.

Her eyes settled on Amy. Amy's eyes were wide open, gazing blankly into the grainy darkness of the room. Silent tears coursed down her pale face.

Beth turned away embarrassed by the tears, uncomfortable that there was nothing she could do to get closer to Amy. Uncomfortable that, at the moment, she had no desire to get closer to Amy — or to help her. What is happening to us, she asked herself. It's like we're challenging each other to break the circle of friends. Can this really be because of the eye? Or is it just us?

Well, whatever the reason, Beth couldn't help wishing that the eye hadn't come along to complicate things. Deep inside, something niggled at her. It was telling her there was trouble brewing. What form it would take was impossible for her to judge.

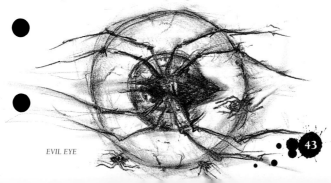

Chapter 4

Daisy and Ashleigh lounged on Daisy's bed. Various bags and packets spewed their contents across the bed and on to the floor. Daisy wore a black beret perched jauntily on her head. A label with a bar code hung down her face like a bizarre earring. Toby, Ashleigh's brother, was in the corner of the room fiddling with an old tape deck.

"Well," said Daisy, "that little spending spree leaves me with hardly a penny for the weekend!"

"You've got some great stuff, though. Won't your mum give you an advance on your allowance?"

"Fat chance! I've had three weeks ahead already." Daisy pushed a bag to the floor.

"Ah! Maybe one of the others will lend you some? Beth must be rolling in it with her job — lucky cow!"

"I was rather hoping to give them a miss this weekend." Daisy rolled onto her back. "They're really getting on my nerves. Always arguing, always moaning — it's like we've got nothing in common except..." She stopped speaking abruptly.

"Yeah? Except what?"

"Oh, I don't know." Daisy blushed uncomfortably. "What're you doing this weekend, Ash?"

"We've got to go visit some old college friend of Dad's. Means they'll sit around boozing and rabbiting on. I'll have to pretend

I'm interested in their reminiscences and It," she jerked her thumb towards Toby, "It'll watch telly until It falls asleep."

"Don't call me It," mumbled Toby.

"And it's Hallowe'en, Saturday night. I bet it'll be brilliant at Tiger's!"

"You hate Tiger's!"

"I know, but Hallowe'en will be fun with everyone dressed up — I bet the atmosphere'll be excellent."

"Hallowe'en," murmured Daisy. "Hallowe'en's just make-believe — voodoo for babies."

"Ah well," Ashleigh shrugged. "I am just a baby at heart. So you won't be going then? I thought you'd go for it as the beautiful Un-Dead Lucy, from *Dracula*!"

"Oh I don't know! I just don't know." Daisy pushed her beret from her head and rubbed at her hair where it had gone flat. "Sometimes I feel like I'm drowning in my own thoughts! Do you know what I mean, Ash?"

"Can't say I do really. Maybe you do need a break from the other three. You guys do live in each others' pockets. It's like you're not that keen on each other but you're determined to torture each other anyway."

"We've known each other since we were little — we're — we're bound together," Daisy paused. "More than ever now."

Ashleigh glanced at her watch. "I guess Mum'll be home from work by now, we should make tracks. Get yourself together Toby, we're off." She turned to Daisy. "Look, Daisy, is there something you're not telling me? It's not like you to keep talking in all these meaningful riddles — you've been doing it all half-term. Has something happened?" She glanced at Toby, then, seeing he was still engrossed, "Is it Amy? She's not pregnant is she?"

"Pregnant! Amy? God no!"

"Okay, okay! Settle down!"

Daisy pressed her hands over her eyes. Then she looked at Ashleigh intently. "I've got something to show you," she said in a hoarse voice.

"Yeah?" Ashleigh was getting impatient. It was Daisy's turn to glance at Toby. Ashleigh was quick on the uptake. "Toby! Aren't you ready yet? Where's your coat? Do you need the loo?"

"Stop behaving like you're my mother." Toby glared angrily at his sister. "I know you just want to get rid of me so's Daisy and you can talk about getting pregnant!"

Ashleigh giggled. "Oh for heaven's sake Toby! Don't be daft!"

Toby stalked from the room.

"Well?" Ashleigh was still laughing.

Daisy moved quickly across the room. She fell to her knees and scrabbled around underneath her desk. Carefully Daisy pulled up a corner of carpet and eased her fingers between a gap in the floorboards. She lifted out a small box.

Turning on her knees she held the box so

that Ashleigh could see it. Gently she lifted the lid.

Ashleigh peered down at the box. "What is it? It's weird, kind of creepy."

"It's the eye," muttered Daisy. "It's Granta's eye."

"That eye from the museum? Oh my — good grief!" Ashleigh reached towards the dark jewel. Daisy snatched the box away from her and shoved it back in its hiding place.

"No!" she said. "It's evil, Ash."

"What kind of evil?" whispered Ashleigh, the image of the eye still glowing in her mind.

"I don't know. All I can say is that we've all been acting so strange since Amy stole it. Since we touched it!"

"Couldn't that just be guilty conscience? I mean, it's a fairly dramatic thing to have done. There was another article about it in the local paper this morning."

"There was? What did it say?"

"I didn't really read it. It was by that curator guy — he's an expert in Instata culture. But the article doesn't really matter. The point is, that eye was stolen a couple of weeks ago now, and the papers are still full of it. You're all bound to feel guilty and jumpy. You've got a guilty conscience, that's all. Get rid of it Daisy. Just get rid of it!"

Daisy was about to reply when a cough startled them. They had forgotten about Toby. He stood, arms folded, leaning against the doorframe. "Ready then, Ash?"

"I'm ready." Ashleigh glared at her brother. "What are you up to, creep?"

"Nothing." He gave a wicked grin. "I don't have a guilty conscience!" So saying, he spun on his heel and walked out.

"Just ignore him." Ashleigh touched Daisy's arm. "He's a pest. Do as I say Daisy, get rid of it."

Daisy shrugged. "Okay," she said.

"Now where's the brat gone?" said Ashleigh, her hand resting on the front door knob. She was just about to yell, when Toby came trotting down the stairs, his hands in his pockets. "Where were you?"

"I went to the loo like you told me, Mummy!"

"Oh, get out of here!" Ashleigh cupped the back of his head in her hand and gave him a little shove out of the door. "Have a good one, Daisy! Enjoy Hallowe'en! See you at school on Monday. Remember what I said!"

But Daisy's mind had already reverted back upstairs to her bedroom with the eye. What was the eye doing to them? It wasn't just guilt. After all, Amy was the only one who'd really done anything wrong — and she still didn't seem worried about it in the slightest. Even Kerima was ratty, getting irritated and angry with everyone, and Kerima really was the most easy-going person in the world.

"Maybe the eye is just an excuse," she said out loud. Her words echoed in the chilly lobby of her house. Maybe, maybe, maybe...maybe not.

Then Daisy remembered the article in the paper Ashleigh had mentioned. She had to know what it said.

She grabbed her coat and ran along the pavement. It was five thirty and already dark. Daisy was so distracted, she wouldn't have noticed the few passers-by even if it had been midday.

The corner shop had sold out of the local newspaper — they only kept a few copies, not much demand and all that. Daisy thanked them ungraciously.

Out on the street, Daisy hesitated. This was the only shop in the small parade of shops that sold newspapers. It was another fifteen minutes into the town centre. She could walk back home and nip round to Ashleigh's, have a look at their copy. But then Ashleigh's family were probably rushing around getting ready to go off. Besides, she didn't want Ashleigh to think she was completely obsessed with the eye, because she wasn't. She just needed to read the article.

Slowly she trudged towards town. Stars already dotted the sky and a white halo encircled the moon. Beth was probably working at the Coffee Stop. She glanced in the steamy window as she walked past. Sure enough, she saw Beth leaning over a table of four middle-aged shoppers, handing out tea and cakes. As she stood up she grinned at them and said something. The shoppers all laughed.

Beth was still making people laugh. She seemed all right, thought Daisy.

She walked quickly past the Coffee Stop before Beth saw her. What an idiot she had been to volunteer to look after the eye. It was hardly surprising it was getting to her. The wretched thing was under the carpet of her bedroom for heaven's sake. Ashleigh was right, she should get rid of the rotten thing. Dump it for once and for all.

Some ten minutes later, Daisy burst into the Coffee Stop in a flurry of cold air. The shoppers had already demolished their cakes and tea, and were getting up to leave. Daisy saw the size of the tip on the table — no wonder that Beth seemed to be able to buy whatever she wanted.

Everyone in the cafe paused for a moment to see who had entered so hurriedly. Seeing Daisy their interest faded as quickly as it had flared.

Beth smiled at her. "Daisy! What's new? You're kind of," she looked Daisy up and down, "wild."

"What's *the* news more like!" said Daisy. "Have you seen this?" She thrust the paper at Beth. Beth took a step back. Greasy Paulo had moved nearer and was watching and listening to every word.

"Why don't you take a seat and have a coffee, Daisy. You look like you need one. It's on me!" She made a show of slamming some money from the tip left by the shoppers back onto the table and making sure Paulo saw and heard exactly what went on. "I'll just wipe that table for you."

Daisy sat where she was told, newspaper still held tightly in her hand. "Now then," Beth placed the coffee on the table, "what are you on about?"

"There's an article in the paper about the eye — about Granta."

"Yeah — well, it's caused quite a stir that robbery. A lot of people coming into the Coffee Stop are still talking about it. No one can believe it's vanished into thin air. It's hardly surprising the paper's still harping on about the crime of the century."

"It's not about the crime, it's about..."

"Beth, if you're going to stand chatting to your sweet little friend, you might just as well take your break — so I don't have to pay for your social life!"

"Okay Paulo — generosity's your middle name!"

"Carry on like that and your break will be permanent!"

Beth sat down opposite Daisy. "Right little charmer, isn't he!" Beth pulled the paper towards her and scanned the article.

'Police continue to be baffled by the audacious crime carried out at Stonybrook Museum two weeks ago. Our reporter visited Mike Todd, assistant curator at the Museum, an expert on Instata customs and beliefs, and discovered that, by taking the eye from the infamous Granta icon, our burglar may have unleashed more forces than those of the Law!'

Beth cocked an eyebrow at Daisy. "Mike Todd? That's our hunky but dull lecturer isn't it?"

"Just read," said Daisy tersely.

Beth scanned the preamble and then read what Mr Todd had to say.

'The Instata invested all their icons with magical powers — some good, some bad, all forceful. Granta, as keeper of human fears, was the strongest and most revered of their gods. He was therefore the most heavily protected by magic.

'The Instata believed that he had it in his power to take away any fears that preyed on their people but, most importantly, if he was displeased with his people he could unleash the most horrendous fears to torture their minds. Many people who crossed Granta or trivialised his powers would, quite simply, go mad with fear.

'Now, I'm not saying that our thief is insane by now. However, it is my opinion, based on my own knowledge and experience of the Instata and other such incidents of desecration, that the burglar and anyone else who has come into direct contact with the eye, could be in grave danger. These Indians made serious magic. I would urge whoever has the eye to restore it to its rightful place as a matter of urgency. Only then do they stand a chance of releasing themselves from Granta's power.'

There followed a list of Strange But True

stories linked to the Instata. An archaeologist who had taken a jewel out of an Instata Temple and attempted to smuggle it home had been paralysed from the neck down in an inexplicable bicycle accident. The Temple was dedicated to Anstiti, goddess of life and vitality. A cleaner in a Brazilian museum who had accidentally knocked the head off a statue of Branit, god of wisdom, was decapitated by the wing of a plane. Beth read a few such examples and pushed the paper away again.

She could not quite bring herself to meet Daisy's eyes.

"Yeah. So what?"

"So we've got Granta's eye! That's so what!"

Daisy suddenly realised how weary Beth looked. Crescent moon-shaped bruises shone beneath both her eyes. "Look, Daisy, are you really surprised? I'm not! But there's not a whole lot we can do about it all now — except not get frightened — and not get silly. My guess is this is all just a local paper drumming up a thrilling story out of a pretty tenuous legend. You saw Mike Todd, they probably paid him to say that stuff. Even if they didn't, just because he says it doesn't make it true. Besides, we just have to live with it."

"Yes, but for how much longer!"

"Oh don't be such a drama queen, Daisy, that's my role, remember."

At that instant, the door flew open and Amy breezed in. She saw Daisy and Beth immediately. "Great!" she said. "Have you...?" then she saw the newspaper. "Ah!" she grinned, "I can see you have! What a hoot!"

"Do all your friends have to make such — how you say — positive entrances, Beth?" Paulo towered above them.

"Sorry Paulo! Can I have another five — I promise these two will buy two more coffees."

"Mmmm, and some cake!" said Amy.

Paulo sighed and shrugged.

A halo of mist from the cold night air gave Amy an other-worldly appearance. She slid into the red plastic bench seat next to Daisy, pulling off her black scarf and denim jacket. She leant across Daisy and drew the shape of an eye on the window in the condensation.

"This is it then! Let's test the power of the eye!"

"What do you mean?" Daisy pushed Amy's scarf off her lap and rubbed her shoulder against the now trickling image on the window.

"Come on, if what the paper says is true, we're all vulnerable to the eye's evil powers. Tomorrow's Hallowe'en — the night of spirits and ghosts and ghouls — the ideal night for us to challenge it to do its worst! We can find out if this load of tripe is true!"

"I still don't understand what you mean." Daisy spoke quietly. Amy waited for Carrie, another waitress, to put their order on the table.

"Bring the eye to Kerima's tomorrow before we set off to Tiger's and we can challenge it to do its worst. It'll really add to the atmosphere, it'll be brilliant."

"I think you'll find that the magic we're dealing with in the eye is very different to that associated with Hallowe'en." Beth spoke matter-of-factly.

"Oh trust you to put a dampener on things!" Amy didn't seem at all perturbed by Beth's comments. Her eyes were shining and her cheeks were flushed. "It's the atmosphere that counts — this is the closest we can get to real fear, real magic, not just dressing up! It's still probably a load of nonsense, but we might as well make the most of it."

"I think you're already going mad," said Daisy. "Either that, or I am."

"Well," said Beth, "I'm game."

"You are? Yes, excellent!" said Amy. Daisy was clearly horrified.

"I, I..."

"What have we got to lose?" Beth hissed at Daisy. Just our minds, she thought to herself. But she said nothing. Instead, she got to her feet, "I'm going back to work. I'll see you tomorrow at Kerima's at about nine. Don't forget to dress up."

She walked slowly away.

"She doesn't seem very enthusiastic," said Amy. "Ah well, at least she agreed!"

"Well I don't. You can count me out." Daisy folded her arms. "I bet Kerima hasn't agreed."

"Leave Kerima to me. Just bring the eye tomorrow, and your good self of course." Amy grinned.

"No," said Daisy. "I'm getting rid of the eye. I'm not coming tomorrow. I've had enough! Anyway, I don't have any money."

Beth had reappeared, cloth in hand, "I'll lend, no, I'll give you the money!"

"Well I'm not coming!"

"Suit yourself," said Amy. "I bet you'll be there. See ya! Oh, and by the way, thanks for the coffee and cake."

Before Daisy could protest, Amy was away and out of the door.

Chapter 5

Amy applied a final round of lip liner and pressed blood-red lips together. She was the Devil. Her chalk-white cheeks glowed dully from under the black hood, her darkened eyes like two malevolent jewels pressed into her face. Jewels dripping black blood.

Her black cloak swept the ground, swirling at her feet. As she moved, folds of the cloth opened to reveal flames of hellfire licking up her body. For an instant, hot and cold flushes of panic rose inside her. The flames seemed to come alive, flickering up her costume. Amy dropped her hands to touch the fire. Gasping she snatched her fingers away from the searing heat.

Her heart pounded like an urgent fist trying to break out of her ribcage. She spun round and rushed for the door. Got to get out of here! A voice inside her screamed. Get away from the fire!

Get a grip! She told herself.

Get a grip.

She shut her eyes, fighting to dispel the images of fire from her mind. She thought so often of Ben. His death so frequently haunted her nightmares, that sometimes it was difficult to separate reality from imagination. Well, she thought, this is just imagination. Now, she told herself, take a deep breath, open your eyes, and hit the town!

She took a last look at herself in the mirror.

Her heart steadied. A slow smile of satisfaction spread across her lips. She was Amy, Amy the She-Devil.

Beth walked into the room where her mum and dad were watching Saturday night TV. Applause and canned laughter pounded at her ears.

"I'm off, then," she said.

"Okay, love. D'you need a lift?" Her father did not take his eyes from the screen. He burst out laughing at some pun made by the presenter of the quiz show.

Her mum, also laughing, turned to look at Beth. "My goodness, Beth! You're the most glamorous witch I've ever seen!"

Beth glanced down at her costume. A skin-tight silvery grey vest dress barely stretched far enough to cover her bottom. Her long legs were encased in black tights which glowed with flecks of red and silver. A full-length red-lined cloak fell to the floor and could encase or reveal as much as Beth desired.

She had spent ages fixing the long blood-red nails to her own rather chewed ones. Beth, unlike Amy, had gone for flattering make-up. Heavy, yes. Startling certainly. But beautiful. A heavy dark kohl outline highlighted with red, made her eyes huge, demanding and fearsome, and sparkling eye shadow added a hint of the exotic. Instead of her short-crop hair she wore a long black wig.

"You like?" she said, twirling on high stilettos.

"We-ell, like isn't exactly the word!" Her mum said, but she smiled. Her dad turned back to the TV in disgust.

"I'm just popping over to Kerima's, so I don't need a lift. We'll all go on to Tiger's together."

"It's all four of you is it?" her dad said. "Well, heaven help Stonybrook!"

Yes, Beth thought as she left the house, heaven help Stonybrook — and heaven help us.

On her way to Kerima's, Beth passed a group of young kids trick or treating, an anxious adult hovering behind them with a sputtering jack-o'-lantern. A huddle of lads, too old to be subjected to parental supervision, but too young to be going to a place like Tiger's, scattered as she approached and she cackled at them. She began to get into the mood, enjoying the power of pretending to be something other than herself.

It was an ideal night for Hallowe'en. It was cool and crisp and bright, but a slight blur across the stars, and a hint of mist promised a more dramatic fog later. At the moment though, the moon hung in the sky like the pupil of a giant eye.

She smiled to herself. The eye. She had made up her mind what to do. The relief at having taken a decision made her feel light-headed. Let Amy have her fun tonight and then Beth knew what had to be done.

She thought of the article that had wound Daisy up the previous day. A cleaner decapitated, an archaeologist paralysed. Despite the warm folds of her cloak she shivered. Then she gave herself a mental shake.

Honestly! This stuff about the eye, it was probably all nonsense, scary legends that had grown up over the years, people bending events to fit the stories they wanted to create. Just like Hallowe'en really. I mean, she thought, the idea that all the dead come to life on Hallowe'en was absolute nonsense. Probably.

"Isn't Daisy with you?" asked Kerima when she opened the door.

"Not unless she's come as a ghost!" quipped Beth.

"You look good." Kerima spoke without warmth.

"So do you!" Beth went for false enthusiasm. "I like the white look, very dramatic with all the black about."

They started climbing the stairs. Beth was startled when Kerima caught hold of her arm — particularly startled by the force of her grasp. When she turned and saw the look of terror in Kerima's eyes, mild surprise turned to shock. Kerima glanced up the stairs as if to check that no one was listening. "What's happening to us Beth? What's happening? Everyone's acting so strange. It's the eye, I know it is! It's the eye."

"Calm down Kerima, it's not like you..."

"But don't you understand," hissed Kerima, "it's started! I know it has! I — I..." Kerima was twisting her hands together now, as if they were one of those interlocking puzzles that are impossible to undo. "I've seen..."

"What are you two doing? Come on, let's party!" Amy's gruesome head poked round the door at the top of the stairs.

"Hey, Amy! You look amazing! Let's see the rest of you!" Beth pulled at Kerima's arm to get her moving.

I'll catch Kerima later, thought Beth, and tell her my plan. That should calm her down. Meanwhile, Amy's right! Let's party!

"It's nearly ten o'clock! Where can she be?" Kerima sat all scrunched up on the sofa.

"Well, her parentals said she'd left at eight thirty, right?" Kerima nodded at Amy's question. "Well, she's either decided not to come — which she definitely threatened — and has gone off with Ashleigh, or something. Or, more likely, she's been attacked by body snatchers on the way here!"

"What else did she say yesterday, Amy?" Beth's mind was racing: if Daisy wasn't coming, she wouldn't be bringing the eye. Never mind, she could get the eye tomorrow. "Did she say anything about the eye?"

"Nope — just that it was in a good hiding place," said Amy. "Look, why don't we get down to business without her. We've all touched the eye. If all the stories are right, we should have no trouble calling up Granta's powers."

"What, 'come Devil meet us in the darkness',

that sort of thing?" Beth laughed.

"Why not? Come on, it'll just give an edge to the evening. Look at us, if everyone at Tiger's is dressed as effectively as us, it'll be a really wild night. With the power of the eye hanging over us, there's always a chance that it won't just be fun fear, it'll be real!" Amy leapt to her feet.

"Come on!" she cried. "Touch fingertips."

In the centre of the dimly-lit room, the three girls made a curious sight. Beth, the vamp-witch, Amy the she-devil, and Kerima the bride of death.

"Granta!" Amy challenged. "Granta, keeper of human fear, release your power for us on Hallowe'en. We have held your eye. We have looked into your eye. We are not afraid! Do your worst Granta!"

Amy's words seemed to fade into the stillness of the room. The only movement was the slight rise and fall of the girls' chests as they breathed.

Beth was aware of the clammy dampness of Kerima's hand and the dry warmth of Amy's. She knew her own hands were damp. She closed her eyes. Immediately she saw a picture of the eye glowing darkly in her mind. Her skin tickled — like a spider was running across her arms, she thought. Her mouth was dry and her head throbbed in the silence. Soon, soon, this, whatever it is, will be over. Soon, I will...

A thud seemed to rock the whole room. Kerima let out a short shriek and Beth gasped.

"Hello!"

The girls had already dropped hands when the door crashed open. They all turned towards the door, their horror and surprise at being disturbed neatly masked by fancy dress make-up.

Beth felt a reluctance to relinquish the feeling that had overcome her as they'd held hands and called up Granta. She had begun to feel safe. Safe to give herself up to the protection of fear. She had suddenly known that if she did surrender herself to the feeling, she would avoid a serious battle. Where that knowledge came from, she did not know. It was as though it had been fed into her mind by a power beyond her control. A power that said: *it's safer to be with me than against me.*

What was clear was that the alternative would be like trying to climb a sheer rock face not just without a rope, but with those ludicrous stilettos currently on her feet.

But, as she gazed at the figure in the doorway through the haze of her trance, she knew she had to fight. Who else was there? Everyone else was succumbing to the power. The power of the eye. Beth instinctively knew she must do whatever was necessary.

The realisation of this was like a metal band around her head getting tighter and tighter, squeezing out the feelings of relief and certainty she had felt earlier. It was all she could do to stop herself falling to her knees and clutching at her head. She thought of Kerima's and Daisy's description of Amy falling to her knees in Tiger's. Had Amy already fought this battle — and lost?

"What *are* you up to? On second thoughts, don't tell me, I don't even want to guess!" None of the girls moved as Kerima's mum continued to talk. "Dad's offering to take you all over to your disco — he's popping to the video shop. But it'll have to be now. Where's Daisy, by the way?"

"Daisy's not coming," said Amy.

"That's right," said Kerima, "and thank Dad for the lift offer, but I think we'll walk. That's half the fun of Hallowe'en." Kerima's voice was quiet, but not shaky. Considering the state she was in only a short while ago, thought Beth, she'd got herself well under control. Her mum looked at them all with a slightly bemused air.

"Suit yourselves," she said. "I warn you, the fog has really come down — it's very murky out there. Wrap up warm!" Then she laughed, "mind you, with the cold blood of the un-dead, I don't suppose such practicalities concern you."

"We'll be fine, Mrs S," Amy smiled. Beth and Kerima voiced their agreement.

"Besides," said Beth, "there's always a distinctly human amount of sweat generated on a good night at Tiger's!" They all laughed.

"Well, Kerima's dad will be there to pick you all up on the dot of 12.30 — please don't keep him hanging around."

Amy was irrepressible as the three made their way to Tiger's through the foggy streets. She was doing her impression of a TV documentary narrator.

"Witness the stillness and the silent fear of passers-by as the three immortals make their way to their destiny. But what will that destiny be? Will they cause havoc and mayhem? Will their powers overcome them? Or will they, quite simply, lose their minds? We follow them on their journey and piece together their mysterious story!"

By contrast, Beth was an extremely quiet and depressed immortal.

Her mind rattled with thoughts that refused to go away. Where was Daisy? It seemed mighty strange to her that Daisy had left home and never arrived at Kerima's. She must have gone out with Ashleigh. But there was a nagging doubt in Beth's mind. She had felt certain that Daisy, despite her anger in the Coffee Stop, would turn up, eye in pocket.

"Let's give the shortcut through the graveyard a miss." Kerima swept along in her ghostly white gown. "It's always like Clapham Junction on Hallowe'en!"

Beth laughed, "You're right. It's the one night of the year I actually feel safe there!"

"Unless Steve Jenkins is lurking behind a gravestone!" Steve Jenkins was the class anorak and Amy couldn't stand to be within a hundred metres of him.

"Knowing him he'd be dressed as Batman!" said Kerima. Then she stopped walking, forcing the others to slow down and finally to stop altogether.

"What's up?" asked Beth shivering. "Let's make tracks, Kerima, we're late already. I feel like dancing to warm myself up — I'm freezing to death!"

"Look, I know you'll think I'm...Listen." Kerima spoke quietly.

Dutifully Beth and Amy listened, holding themselves stiffly against the dank chill of the night. They were still on residential streets and the sound of the traffic from the main road was muffled. The only sounds were a few cries from surrounding streets and the odd firecracker. With the fog, it was almost impossible to judge directions and distances of the noises.

"Yes?" said Amy impatiently. "What are we supposed to be hearing?"

"Beth, did you hear anything?"

"Nope," said Beth. "Not a dicky bird, sorry Kerima."

"I keep hearing footsteps." The other two groaned. "I know you think I'm being stupid but I'm sure, and the bushes back there on the edge of the common — I heard them rustling."

"Well, the bushes rustling was probably my dicky bird!" said Beth.

"And," said Amy, "the footsteps were

probably our own — particularly since they seem to have stopped now we have!"

"I know I heard something," said Kerima. "And I knew you wouldn't believe me!"

"Oh, for heaven's sake Kerima, you're supposed to hear things — it's Hallowe'en!"

"Well, the sooner we get to Tiger's the better," said Beth. She smiled at Kerima, and they all set off once more.

Beth was still nervous and couldn't stop herself from glancing back towards the common. The inky shadows clustered along the edge resembled hunched figures in the darkness and fog. And it would be oh, so easy, to believe that one of them was moving. Maybe even following them. She turned her head firmly towards Tiger's. She would not let her imagination run away with her: there was enough to deal with, without an over-active imagination.

They began to bump into several of their classmates, and Beth, who thanks to her job at the Coffee Stop, was well-known in Stonybrook, was hailed by sundry ghosts, ghouls, Frankensteins and Draculas.

At last they joined the queue for Tiger's. Since they were so late the queue wasn't too bad. Inside, the heavy thud of the bass pummelled at their ears and they grinned at each other in expectation. The music at Tiger's was always really good and had them all dancing in no time. Once they were inside all their everyday worries vanished as they lost themselves in the music.

Beth glanced around but couldn't see Daisy. Tomorrow she would go round to Daisy's and sort it out. But still the doubt niggled at her. What if something had happened to Daisy? As she moved towards the dance floor, with the other eager ravers, she asked herself just what could have happened to Daisy? Decapitated by an aeroplane — well, hardly! Waylaid by unforeseen circumstances...

Soon, her body and mind gave themselves up to the music. It throbbed within her, as she twisted and swayed, enjoying the swirl of her long cloak. Pulsing lights around them were like a giant kaleidoscope of colour. It felt so good to lose herself in the music, rather than be wrestling with her thoughts.

She flirted outrageously with a couple of blokes who came in the Coffee Stop every so often, dancing close to them and laughing loudly at their jokes.

They moved away from the dance floor to catch their breath and watch the action from the safety of a bar stool. She accepted their offer of a drink. They were too old for her taste — early twenties, but she enjoyed the envious looks of the other girls. She was even tempted to try the bottle of vodka they were passing round. They tried to entice her into a swig but she had no desire to drink vodka. She had tried it once before at home and hated the sour aftertaste. Although her parents sometimes allowed her a glass of wine she didn't really like the stuff. One of the few things she, Amy, Kerima and Daisy did still have in common, she thought.

She let the two lads' conversation drift into the din of the music and searched the room for the others. Still no sign of Daisy, and Kerima had disappeared. Amy wasn't difficult to spot. She was dancing wildly with Danny King, of all people.

Danny hadn't been able to resist enhancing his good looks. Mind you, even a plastic surgeon with a blunt scalpel would struggle to damage his perfect nose and cheekbones. His blonde hair was slicked back. He had darkened his eyes with kohl and dressed himself up in a tux with a high-necked Dracula cloak. White pointed fangs twinkled on his bottom lip. He looked good enough to be eaten by and Amy was certainly making a major play to be first on the menu.

Beth had never seen Amy dance that way before — if she didn't know better, she would have believed that Amy had drunk a few shots of the vodka. But she knew that Amy was high on the atmosphere, on adrenaline — and on the power of Granta.

Beth turned her attention back to her two older men. They were no longer at her side but had moved along the bar to Dizzy Cobb. Dizzy was dressed in scarlet — all teeth and cleavage thought Beth. One of the guys had his arm draped carelessly around her shoulders and as she leant back into it, his fingers ran up and down her bare arm. The guy happened to catch Beth's eye and he shrugged and gave a sort of half grin. Beth cocked a mocking eyebrow, which made him laugh. It also made Dizzy look directly at her. She gave Beth the queen of smug looks, and clung tighter to the guy's arm.

"You're welcome!" muttered Beth under her breath.

She spotted Kerima on the dance floor now. Another seriously out of control dancer, thought Beth. Excellent! She leapt to her feet, ready for another dance. There was something extraordinarily exhilarating about dancing with a bunch of freaks and weirdos. She headed for Kerima but had to pass Amy and Danny on her way through. She paused long enough for Danny to brush her ear with those little teeth and mutter something completely unintelligible into it, and for Amy to give her a discreet thumbs up sign.

Moving on through the throng of bodies, she felt a hand grip her hard on the arm.

Something about the force of the fingers digging into her flesh set her pulse racing. She tried to twist round to see who it was. For an instant, pressed in the squeeze of moving bodies, all she could see were unknown faces. The next moment, she knew who that urgent hand belonged to. It was a sight that sent her heart lurching up to her throat and made her mouth dry.

The music suddenly sounded hollow and

distant. All she could see was the face she knew so well, completely transformed by dirt and scratches.

And by something else.

Fear.

It was Daisy.

But a Daisy she had never seen before.

Chapter 6

Despite the jostling of the dancers all around her there was no possibility of becoming separated from Daisy. Her grip was too tight. The two girls didn't lose eye contact, but neither tried to speak.

Beth danced backwards towards the exit. She managed to take Daisy's free hand in her own, but still Daisy did not release her arm. Beth was so confused by Daisy's appearance that she couldn't think straight. She could only concentrate on trying to get somewhere less crowded. Somewhere she could begin to ask the millions of questions that clamoured in her mind.

After what seemed like forever, they reached the edge of the dance floor and moved out into the corridor, still clinging to each other. A constant mill of people pressed along the corridor in both directions, but at least the pounding music wasn't quite as overpowering here.

"What? What is it, Daisy? What's the matter? What's happened?" Beth was yelling at Daisy. Daisy's mouth worked, but nothing came out. "Yes?" cried Beth. It was difficult to sound encouraging when you were screeching at the top of your voice.

She reviewed Daisy's state once more and felt the panic rise within her. Considering the weird and wonderful costumes, Daisy didn't look out of place. She looked like she had just crawled out of the grave. Beth knew this wasn't a fancy dress effect, this was for real. "Are you hurt?" she tried lowering her voice a fraction. Daisy managed to shake her head. Her eyes began to dart backwards and forwards as if she were being hunted. She let go of Beth's arm. It looked as if she would run away. Beth grabbed her shoulders. "Talk to me Daisy. Tell me what's happened. Is it the eye?" Daisy's wild eyes steadied for a moment and as she stared hard at Beth, a single tear rolled down her mud-streaked cheek. She nodded slowly, and then shook her head jerkily.

"You must calm down! You must tell me. Look, don't panic. Go home. I'll come tomorrow. I know what to do about the eye. If the eye is making us behave like this, I know how to stop it. Give it to me tomorrow. We can get rid of it!"

Beth's words seemed to agitate Daisy even more. She pulled away from Beth, pushing her back against the wall so hard that she lost her footing and slid down towards the ground. She quickly steadied herself with a hand and staggered back up to full height just in time to see Daisy disappearing out of a fire exit further along the corridor.

She elbowed her way through the people, ignoring the yells and complaints and stepped out through the door.

The force of the cold night air slammed into her like one of the swing doors at the Coffee

Stop. She gasped; the misty air filled her lungs, making her want to cough. The fog swirled around her as if to cover Daisy's departure. She stood for a moment, trying to peer through the blanket of grey. She could see nothing except parked cars.

She was trembling, not from cold, from shock. What should she do? Her mind was blank. She'd go back, go back and find the other two, then they would decide.

She turned to go back inside, but the door had closed behind her and it couldn't be opened from the outside. The decision, it seemed, had been made for her. Pulling her cloak tightly around her and swallowing hard, she set off across the car park.

"Daisy! Daisy!" her tentative voice disappeared into the fog. And so did Beth, exchanging the bright lights and noise of Tiger's for the eerie quiet of the foggy night. She must find Daisy and, if she could not find her, she must go to Daisy's parents and warn them something had happened to Daisy. Something dreadful.

Amy was having a whale of a time! She had never taken any notice of Danny King before. In fact, she had never been *that* interested in any of the boys she knew — particularly not in their school. But here she was, moving close to Danny, and loving it. She rested her cheek against his chest, feeling the damp heat from his body. This was fun, she thought. And, what's more, he smelt good too! Maybe she would develop a keener interest in the opposite sex.

There had been Ben, of course, and his mates. But that was different. Her fascination with Ben had been more akin to Ashleigh's little brother's attempts to get involved in Ashleigh's life — well, to listen in on her life and the lives of her friends. And she had certainly listened in on Ben's life and had known what was going on in it.

Danny's hands moved across her back, pulling her even tighter to him. She tried to think just about Danny, lose her other thoughts in the noise and lights of Tiger's. But that insistent voice inside her head would not be quiet. 'You knew,' it said. 'You knew, but you did not save him, did you? You could have saved him. You *should* have saved him.'

Kerima had moved to the balcony above the dance floor. She gazed down at the mêlée. Despite the hundred or so people on the dance floor, it was impossible for her eyes not to keep focusing on Danny and Amy. She hated them both at that moment. She gripped her glass in her hand. How could Amy do this to her? How could Danny humiliate her like this?

She didn't feel any pain immediately. She just sensed something was wrong but she wasn't sure what. It was the gasp of horror from the witch next to her that made Kerima glance down.

She saw a bright red patch growing down the front of her dress. Too bright for blood, she thought. Besides, blood would not be unusual on Hallowe'en. The stain was spreading, though. Spreading across her chest and stomach. Again, quite fitting for Hallowe'en, she thought.

"Oh my god!" she heard the girl next to her cry. "Your hand! Look at your hand!"

Kerima looked at her hand and the broken glass clasped in it. She looked down at the blood spattering over the front of her beautiful white dress. She looked up again at the girl who was staring at her, and at the growing group of people who couldn't decide whether to move away or to approach her. She looked at them and she screamed.

Daisy ran. On and on and on through the fog not really knowing where she was going, like Scarlett O'Hara's nightmare in *Gone With the Wind*. She wanted to get home and stay there. She wanted to go to bed and rest. Go to bed and sleep, let mum and dad look after her. Sleep, so that when she woke up all of this would be over.

Before she crawled into bed, she would take a last look under her desk, under the carpet, under the floorboards. Perhaps the eye would be there this time.

That's how the evening had started. And

however many times she had looked, however many times she went over it all in her mind, she could not make the eye reappear. It was gone. Disappeared. Vanished.

She stopped running, letting the fog engulf her. She was momentarily surprised to see where she was. But then she knew it was meant to be. She looked at the smooth black surface of the lake, and slowly moved towards it.

When she'd realised that the eye wasn't there, her thoughts had turned to Beth and Amy. She had threatened to get rid of the eye — to dump it. Maybe they had panicked. Perhaps one of them had taken it. But how? No one knew where she had hidden the eye. Only Ashleigh. And Ashleigh wasn't involved in this. She had gone away for the weekend with her parents. Anyway, why would she want to take the eye? No, it had to be one of the others.

She tried to sequence the events in her mind but her mind wasn't working properly. She couldn't remember when she had last looked at the eye. She couldn't remember who had visited her house and when they had visited her. The only thing she really knew was that the disappearance of the eye was a catastrophe. She did not know why, she just felt it deep inside.

Then she started to believe the others were ganging up on her. Hadn't Beth suddenly started supporting Amy, when she had been so against the eye that first evening at Kerima's? Somehow, some way they had taken the eye.

They'd tricked her. For a moment she told herself this was madness. Of course they wouldn't have done that! But she couldn't calm herself. She knew she had to find them, follow them, see what they were up to.

And that's just what she had done. But she had got lost. Lost in bushes and brambles. Lost — she did not know where. All she knew was that her mind seemed to be out of control. Thoughts of death and dying kept pounding at her.

When at last she had found Tiger's it hadn't been real for her. Beth trying to talk to her had made Daisy realise they were all mad. All going mad. She wanted to get out of Tiger's, get away from the madness. But it stayed with her.

Now she looked at the lake. She stood at the water's edge, the dark liquid touching the ends of her shoes. She had no control over her limbs. Something was steering her body as if by remote control.

But there was nothing remote about her heart pounding inside her chest. Nothing remote about her mind screaming with terror as the lake drew her in. Powerless to stop herself, she entered the black depths of the water. This was her fate.

The voices were distant and almost meaningless. "She'll need stitches." "Hang on, I think she's going to faint." "Who'd have thought such a small cut would produce so much blood?" "She's as white as a ghost — oops, sorry!" Music, even more remote than the voices, pounded in Kerima's head.

Then she felt a coat being pulled roughly around her shoulders. It was her dad. Someone had called her dad.

"Come on," he was saying. "Let's get you to Casualty. Where are the others?"

Kerima was shaking violently. She felt so cold, as if every ounce of blood had drained out of her system and been replaced by liquid ice. She clung tightly to her dad. She knew he was waiting for an answer but she couldn't make her lips move.

Then she heard Amy's voice. "It's okay Mr S. We'll make our own way back. I've already 'phoned home."

"Okay, Amy."

Kerima's dad steered her towards the exit. But not before Kerima caught sight of Danny King and Amy. Their faces seemed to press towards her. Both looked anxious. She didn't need their anxiety — she stared hard at Amy, puzzled by what she was seeing.

"I'll be round to see you tomorrow, Kerima. Take care."

Kerima continued to stare. Horror replaced confusion. She felt vomit rising in her throat.

"There's blood..." she croaked. "Blood!"

"It's alright, sweetheart, you've cut yourself," her dad was saying.

Kerima shook herself, trying to escape her father's grasp. Did no one understand her. Could no one see? There was blood for heaven's sake. Thick, dark, red blood trickling from Amy's eyes. Pouring from her mouth now, and flowing out of her nose. And Amy just stood there, blood streaming down her face, neck and chest.

Kerima's father was pulling her out into the open air. She dragged heavily on him, craning her head back to keep Amy in her line of vision. But Amy had gone.

Kerima bent over in the car park to throw up. The sick spattered down her dress. Sick and blood, she thought. Tears squeezed at her eyes as she coughed. But inside she smiled. She was glad, glad that Amy must be dead.

"Come on, Kerima," her dad wiped her mouth with a tissue and pulled her to him protectively. "Let's get you stitched up and home to bed."

Cold fingers pulled at Daisy, dragging her deeper into the water which was now up to her chest. Her clothes were leaden with water and they pulled her heavily down under the surface. Now it was in her ears, in her eyes, her nose and her mouth. Sticks scratched at her hands, and a piece of slimy weed stuck to her face. She opened her eyes wide to examine the murky depths. She hated water. Why was she here? How did she get here?

Now the water was crushing her, slowly squeezing the air from her lungs. Her chest ached from holding her breath. She opened her mouth to scream for help and swallowed a gulp of water, choking her, drowning her. She began to thrash in the icy depths, trying desperately to regain the surface, but a leaden weight held her down beneath the water. The pull of the water clamped to her ankles like leg-irons, pressing down on her head, bending her under its weight. And there, through the darkness of the lake, glowed the eye. Its unblinking gaze mocked her, taunting her with the knowledge that all this was Granta's doing.

When the rescuing hands grabbed her, pulling her head above the water, she was almost too weak to help. But sheer terror gave her strength. She staggered to her feet, amazed that she was in the shallows of the lake. Hadn't she just been drowning in deep water? Obviously not.

She knew what wet through meant now — she was full of water inside and out. But, more than anything else, she was cold. Her bones ached from it and her teeth were chattering so violently it hurt. She collapsed on the bank of the lake, coughing up water until her throat was raw.

Beth ran for what felt like miles. She had a searing pain in her chest and stomach. Her breath tore at her mouth and throat in short ripping gasps. Sweat stung her eyes. She did not know what drove her to the lake. It was such a bleak place that only a fool would go there at this time of night. A fool, or someone who did not know what they were doing.

Beth had stumbled through the under-growth, tearing her ridiculous cloak on the bushes and brambles. She saw the movement, and heard the thrashing of water: she rushed straight into the lake, grabbing wildly. At first Daisy's limbs slipped from her grasp, but at last she got a firm hold about her shoulders and heaved with all the strength she had left.

Daisy felt someone there with her, stroking her back, pulling her up to sitting position and draping a warm blanket around her. But it was only when Beth spoke that she realised it was her friend who had saved her and that the blanket was Beth's fancy dress cloak. Hallowe'en seemed a whole nightmare ago.

"Daisy? Oh, Daisy, thank god you're all right!"

The girls clung together, sobbing into each others' shoulders. "Daisy, we've got to get you home, got to get you to see a doctor."

"No! No doctors. I'll be alright. Get me home, Beth. Please take me home."

"Okay. Come on. Let's get you to your feet.

You're shivering so! I'm sure you need to see..."

Daisy stopped trying to scramble to her feet. "It was the eye, Beth! It was the eye that made me do it!"

"I know. I know it was, Daisy. We're going to put it back. You're going to give it to me tomorrow, and we'll put it back. To hell with whether we get caught or not. I'll speak to Amy and Kerima and we'll all do it together!"

Daisy let out a heart-rending sob that shook her body even more than the tremors from the cold.

"What?" said Beth, dropping to her knees and looking anxiously into Daisy's face. "What is it? Have you broken something? Is it your legs?"

"Oh, Beth, it's the eye! We can't put it back."

"Yes, yes we can Daisy. It's our only chance. Don't think about it now. Just try not to be frightened. I'm sure Granta is messing with our minds. Don't let him frighten you. We will put the eye back. We will!"

"But you don't understand. I don't have the eye! The eye has gone!"

Daisy's words sank in. Beth pulled Daisy to her feet, "Right," she said, "let's get you home."

As Beth and Daisy struggled back to Daisy's house, the rain started to fall. Beth thanked her lucky stars — at least that would be one less explanation to make.

As they rounded the last street corner, Beth heard a sound which made her start to giggle.

"Why are you laughing?" Daisy whispered.

"The bells," said Beth. "The clocks are just striking midnight on Hallowe'en!" The girls stopped and listened to the deep resonance of each of the twelve chimes. "It's so unreal," said Beth.

Daisy slumped into Beth's shoulder. "Oh, Beth, what are we going to do?" Beth moved slowly towards Daisy's front door, supporting her friend. She felt hollow. All her energy resources were on empty. Her mind had ground to a halt, and her body felt like a boxer's punch-bag.

"I don't know, Daisy. I just don't know."

Chapter 7

It was a more piercing, insistent bell that penetrated Beth's oppressive sleep the following morning. She groaned. Everything felt heavy. Her head, her body — her heart.

She didn't relish the memories of the previous night. They had battered away at her subconscious until twilight.

She knew they had to have a council of war — her, Daisy, Kerima and Amy. Obviously they had to decide what to do.

"Beth, it's for you!" Beth could picture her mum, one foot on the bottom stair, half swinging off the banister as she yelled.

"Okay — I'll take it up here!" Beth dragged herself out of bed. She pulled her T-shirt down her legs a bit, and padded out on to the landing.

"Hello," Beth's voice croaked from sleep. "Oh, it's you. Listen, we've got major problems. We all need to meet up."

"Haven't you heard?"

"What? About Daisy? I was there. How did you know, have you spoken to her? How is she?"

"Wow!" Amy tutted. "Slow down! I haven't got a clue what you're on about. I'm talking about Kerima! Kerima had an accident last night."

"Oh — what! What kind of accident?"

"Beth, hang on. She's alright. At least, she had to have ten stitches in her hand. But her father was a bit funny with me on the 'phone this morning. If we have a pow-wow, we need to leave Kerima out of it for a few days. He said not to visit her — she'd be in touch when she was ready."

Beth struggled to take in what Amy was telling her.

"What did she do to her hand?" demanded Beth.

Amy told Beth what she knew, and at last Beth was able to piece together the events at Tiger's that she had missed while she was pounding through the foggy night and saving Daisy from drowning.

"So what was with Daisy?" asked Amy. "Where did you disappear to?"

"I really can't talk right now. We should meet this after...oh blast! I'm working."

"What time do you finish?"

At last the girls agreed to meet in the shopping mall at five thirty, after Beth's shift. As Beth replaced the receiver, the enormity of the previous evening's events began to sink in.

As if in a trance, she walked back to her bedroom. Keep things in perspective, she told herself. Then, out loud, she said, "Kerima's hand could be, no, was, an accident. Anyone could cut their hand on a broken glass. But what about Daisy? How could Daisy ending up thrashing about in the lake be an accident?" The more she thought about the emotions and events unleashed over the past few weeks, the more uneasy she became.

Anyone watching the two girls sitting on the marble wall around the fountain wouldn't have thought they were friends. Their body language was all wrong. Legs crossed away from each other and arms folded tightly across chests.

"You seem very cool about this, Amy." Beth didn't even bother to mask her irritation.

"What's the point in getting wound up?"

"Aren't you frightened about what's going to happen to you?" Beth glared at Amy. Amy didn't answer, and made a big show of thinking about Beth's question. Beth had to stop herself from prompting an answer. Finally Amy spoke.

"No. I don't care what happens to me. That's the point."

Beth sensed a flicker of anxiety, a hint of self-doubt. But she knew there was no point in pressing Amy. What would it achieve?

"Okay, so you don't care about yourself, but what about the rest of us? What about Daisy and Kerima?"

"Yeah," said Amy, "Daisy's an odd one. I went round to see her, her mum said she was ill — flu, or something. I went up to her room to see her and she just wasn't making sense at all. I think she's delirious. Maybe her midnight dip has given her brain damage!"

"God, you're unbelievable! I can't believe you can joke about this! Don't you understand that if I hadn't turned up, Daisy would be dead? You should have seen her face when I dragged her out of the water! I'll never forget her expression."

"Okay! I'm sorry. I guess it has got to me more than I thought, but just lighten up a bit will you? You keep associating everything with the eye. Why does it all have to be linked to the eye?" Amy wasn't thinking about what she was saying — she was thinking about faces that stick in your memory forever. In particular Ben's face, which so often came to her as a mask of death. She hadn't even seen him dying, but she might just as well have done.

"Look," Amy continued, "I don't agree with you that Daisy's and Kerima's adventures are connected with Granta — if that was the case why hasn't it affected me, or you? If you think it will help to ease your conscience, let's put the wretched eye back. It shouldn't be that difficult. Even if we just leave it somewhere where it can be found."

"You just don't get it do you? Daisy says the eye has gone!" It was the first time Beth felt any of her words had actually made an impact on Amy.

"Gone? What do you mean gone? She didn't say anything to me about it."

"I don't know. Daisy wasn't exactly making sense last night — and from what you say, she's not a whole lot better today."

"Beth?"

"Yes."

Amy looked deep into Beth's eyes.

"Daisy threatened to dump the eye. Throw it

away."

Beth nodded. "Yes, I know."

"If she's done that," Amy hesitated. "If she's dumped it somewhere, we might never find it. We might..."

"Might never find it? Might never be able to put it back? But why should that matter Amy? The eye's powers are a load of nonsense, aren't they? So it doesn't matter if we put it back or not, does it?"

"But I had hoped...I had thought..."

"No, Amy! That's the whole rotten point! You just didn't think! You just got carried away doing what you wanted, behaving like the selfish person you are!" Beth was leaning towards Amy, jerking her finger belligerently in Amy's face. "You said to me that you didn't care about fear — well I don't believe you. I think all of this has been about trying to get away from yourself because you're frightened of something. Well, the game's over, Amy! It's time to face reality! It's time to face up to yourself!"

Amy was staring at her but she was not seeing her. She was seeing Ben, taunting her, telling her she was a creep, a pain in the neck, telling her she couldn't keep a secret. Well, she could! She had! And look where it had got her!

"Leave me alone!" she screamed. "You deserved to die!" She lurched at Beth, who in her eyes was Ben, knocking her back into the fountain and falling on top of her.

A crowd began to gather. People gasped as

the two girls continued to writhe about in the water, pulling at each others' clothes and hair.

At last Beth dragged herself to her feet. "Amy," she screeched. "Amy, for heaven's sake, stop it!" Then she saw all the people staring at them.

"I hate you!" yelled Amy. "Why can't you leave me alone? Leave me alone!" She launched herself at Beth again. Beth drew back her hand and smacked Amy smartly around the face.

Amy staggered slightly. She blinked, and touched her cheek where Beth had slapped her. She looked around at the fountain. The water was squirting out of the mouth of a giant fish, splashing around her and Beth. It was Beth, not Ben. "I...what happened?"

Beth saw two security guards heading through the mall towards them. "Later," she hissed. "Let's get out of here!" She grabbed Amy's sodden sleeve and dragged her out of the fountain. The two girls ran for the swing doors. Beth glanced over her shoulder. The guards hadn't even bothered to give chase but had settled to urge the group of shoppers to resume their own business. Much safer than chasing two screaming girls who had just been wrestling in the fountain — all donations collected and sent to MIND. Very appropriate, thought Beth wryly.

"Let's go back to my place," panted Amy. They had paused on the corner of the street, neither of them too sure what to do next.

"Okay. Is anyone there?" Beth could not face

yet more explanations, it had been hard enough explaining last night. If she came home looking wrecked this evening, her parents would throw the book at her. Mind you, compared to what was happening to her now, her parents throwing the book at her would be a doddle.

They walked briskly. Finally Beth felt calm enough to speak. "I hope there's a good explanation for that little outburst," she said. "Because that's the second drenching I've had in less than twenty four hours. I have to drag one idiot out of water and then lo and behold another idiot — that's you, just in case you hadn't realised — drags me into it!"

Amy smiled weakly, but she didn't speak. Her mind tumbled with images. Kerima being dragged from Tiger's and the weird look on her face as she had turned to stare back at her; dancing with Danny King; wrestling with Beth in the fountain. Life had certainly taken a hectic and unpredictable turn. So many changes. And yet, in reality, nothing had changed. Ben's death would not go away. Could she really have saved him?

"Beth..."

"Yes, Amy."

Through the blur that was beginning to cover her vision, Amy could see that Beth was concerned.

"I don't think..." The words caught in her throat. Why were the words so hard to get out?

Suddenly she realised why. It was the smoke. The smoke that was engulfing her. She groped through the smoke towards Beth, managing to take hold of Beth's wrist. Still she couldn't speak, Beth's lips were moving.

"Amy! Amy, what's happening?"

Amy could hear Beth's words, just. But she knew she was disappearing, fading away. Everything seemed distant and unreal, tiny droplets of cold sweat formed on her upper lip, nose and forehead.

"Can't fight anymore," she croaked. "Find the eye, Beth. Stop..." Before the fire engulfed her, Amy heard Beth's words fading away.

"You've got to fight! Come back here Amy, come back! Whatever's happening in your head is not real! Fight it! It's not real!"

But the flames crackled up around her, and she felt too overwhelmed to push them away this time. Giving herself up to them would be easier. Wouldn't it?

The searing heat began to close in on her. Smoke curled around her, filling her lungs, choking her. She began to cough. Fierce, throat-tearing coughs that dragged the smoke even deeper into her chest. She raised her hand to wipe the sweat out of her eyes and saw the flesh was melting away from the bones. It was bubbling up and breaking open like a doll's face in a bonfire. She felt a scream rising inside her.

But there was Ben, coming towards her. Handsome, healthy Ben. Coming to save her from the nightmare. He drew closer, moving through the flames and smoke.

"Help!" she begged. "Save me!"

It was then that the smell hit her nostrils. A rotten, decaying smell that clawed as viciously at her senses as the all encompassing reek of her own burning flesh. She gagged at the sickly-sweet fumes of death. Tears poured down her face. As Ben drew closer, she saw what she already knew.

His flesh was a mass of gaping sores, barely clinging to charred bones. He moved towards her, reaching for her, skin hanging from skeletal fingers.

"No!" she gasped, wrenching the word from deep within her. Pain scorched its way through her body. Pain and fear.

A voice mimicking her own, but sounding like a tape playing on slow, echoed in her ears. "Save me!" On and on and on it echoed.

The black holes that were Ben's eyes forced their way closer and closer to her own face. His mouth moved in a mask, a grotesque caricature of the Ben Amy had once known. He started laughing, his foul breath over her face.

She turned to try and run, but something was holding her back — back to face the monstrous thing behind her. Her legs moved, and she struggled with all her might, but she was glued to the spot.

She stopped fighting. Slowly she turned round. Ben's rotting fingers clawed at her, holding her still. She hit at the hand, finally grabbing hold of it to try and release its grip. Slimy flesh slipped off into her fingers.

She was screaming now. Screaming straight into Ben's face, except it wasn't Ben's face. It was Granta's. Eye's gleaming, tongue dangling, saliva splashing across her face.

Granta was laughing at her, too. Roaring directly into her mind without having to speak. *This is fear, Amy! This is your fear! Did you kill Ben? Yes, you killed him!*

Amy's head pounded, her heart felt like it was exploding in her chest. She writhed against the force that held her down. She couldn't take anymore! No more!

Then, nothing. Just like that. Emptiness.

Beth sat in the hospital corridor. Poor, poor Amy. Beth could not think straight. What should she do now? What could she do now? She knew she had to take action. But with the eye missing and Daisy unwilling or unable to talk about it, it was impossible to know where to start.

Watching Amy collapse had absolutely shattered her. How could it happen? What logical explanation could there be for a perfectly healthy fifteen year-old to start ranting and raving as if she were possessed by malevolent spirits? The possible truth was too dreadful to think about. In the stuffy hospital corridor, Beth watched nurses, doctors, patients, their friends and visitors, shuffle and bustle. She so wanted there to be a simple explanation but a heavy dread weighed down on her. Nothing was simple anymore.

Beth had quickly realised that Amy was hallucinating — and she was almost certain that the same thing had happened in the shopping mall. She tried to get through to Amy that whatever she was seeing and feeling was not real.

For a moment, Beth thought she had reached Amy and got her to believe it was all in her head. If this was to do with the eye, then that had to be the answer, surely? Wasn't that what Granta did? He messed with your mind — realised your worst fears. To fight his power surely you had to convince yourself it wasn't real. But Amy was strong and she had obviously fought — and lost. What did that mean for the rest of them?

It had been all Beth could do to hang on to her and stop her from running out in front of a car. Someone must have phoned the police, and an ambulance had arrived. They strapped Amy into a stretcher. She had knocked a drip tube, so that it sprayed all over her and anyone standing close by. She had grabbed at the hand of one of the paramedics, pulling a glove off. That had really set her screaming. The last Beth had seen of Amy, they injected her with something and she'd stopped in her tracks, floppy like a rag doll. Apparently that's how she still was.

Beth had been interviewed by the police. Again. Half of her kept expecting them to ask her about the eye. But why should they make any connection between a girl collapsing and the eye missing from some Instata icon in a local museum? No one would think to make that kind of connection — even if presented with the facts.

It was just too far-fetched for words.

Perhaps someone should tell Granta that, thought Beth. Excuse me, Granta, but real life isn't like this. Go back to your world and just behave yourself.

At last Amy's dad turned up at the hospital and told Beth to go home.

Her mum rushed to the door when she arrived.

"What happened? How's Amy?"

Beth shrugged. Angrily she dashed the tears from her eyes. "I don't know Mum. They don't know. It could be a fit or something. She's still unconscious. They should know more when she comes round and they've carried out tests."

"Her poor father," murmured Beth's mum. Beth felt like slapping her. What about Amy? What about her, Beth? Then she remembered that her mum couldn't possibly know what was happening. For one mad moment, she thought of telling her mother. Wouldn't it be great to get this all off her chest, tell Mum, feel her arms around her, making it all better.

She stopped herself from blurting out the story of Granta and Granta's eye just in time. Even though she was now convinced of the fact that Granta was playing games with their minds — how would she convince anyone else? Besides, the eye was missing. What could anyone do to help them? She had to face up to the fact that she was on her own. Kerima was refusing to talk to anyone. Daisy would only say she wanted no more to do with the eye and start warbling on about drowning.

Only Beth was hanging on to reality. Hanging on to the fact that if someone did not do something about the eye, life could never be normal again. But what could she do?

Big, fat tears splashed down her face. She felt her mum's arms around her, and heard her warm words, "You've been so brave, love. Your poor friend. Poor you. What you need is a good night's sleep. Thank goodness it's half-term. No work at that wretched café for you tomorrow, and that's final!"

But the arms and the words held no comfort for Beth. She felt a cold core of despair forming inside her. She didn't know what to do. And a good night's sleep was hardly going to solve that.

Chapter 8

"Look, Kerima," Beth spoke slowly and firmly, as if she were speaking to a young child. "I don't think you're hearing me. We're all in trouble here. We've got to stick together."

"Oh, I understand all right!" Kerima's voice was bitter. "Well, I don't want anything else to do with it. I've had it with Granta and the eye. You do what you like, but don't include me." Her bandaged hand rested on top of her duvet. Her good hand fiddled constantly with the pages of a magazine.

"You can't say that."

"I don't care what you say." Kerima turned to look out of her bedroom window.

"Well," Beth's voice was harsh, "you should have thought about that before you decided there was no harm in the eye, before you decided to touch it."

Kerima continued to stare out of the window. Her lips were drawn tight together.

"Look, Kerima," Beth tried to claw back some patience. "I know you've had a shock with your hand and everything. But I know you, I know that you really care about Daisy and me, and poor Amy." Her words certainly got a reaction.

Kerima turned sharply towards her, her mouth curled in a sneer. "I'm glad Amy's dead. Glad, glad, glad! She mocked me, her and

Danny King." The words were like a smack round the face to Beth.

"Dead! What do you mean? Oh no!"

"I saw the blood pouring from her!" continued Kerima. "Well, it's what she deserved!" She shuddered. "It was like she popped. All the blood forcing its way out of her."

"What do you mean?" demanded Beth. "What are you going on about?"

"At Tiger's." Kerima looked haunted, her eyes huge. "When Amy died. I wished it on her."

Beth fought back an urge to crawl under Kerima's sheets and stay there forever. To shut herself off from reality by choice, rather than wait for Granta to catch up with her. Gently, she took Kerima's hand and began to stroke it.

"It's okay, Kerima, Amy's not dead. She's alive and well. You rest now and you'll soon be over this flu. I'll come back and see you in the next couple of days." Kerima's eyes had drifted away, as if she had gone to some distant place where no one could reach her. Beth ached inside.

Beth glanced down at Kerima's limp hand. What she saw made her bite her lip so hard that she drew blood.

She wasn't holding Kerima's hand.

She was holding the largest, most revolting spider she had ever seen. Its black and yellow striped legs were alive with bristling, glistening hairs. Her throat was so tight she could not breathe. She moved her hand tentatively and the thing started to move up her wrist. She could feel it! Her flesh tingled and tried to shrink away from the beast. Every single ounce of her body screamed in disgust and horror.

If she did not get a grip on herself, she would suffocate. Her sight was getting blurred. Her mouth was working, but no words came out, and no air seeped in. It was like somene had shoved a ball of scrunched up paper into her throat.

Still the thing edged its legs over her skin, its dark brightness making a stark contrast against her own pale skin.

She was falling. Falling away from consciousness. Is this how it was for Amy, she heard herself think. Is this how...? How nice it would be to just go with it, let go, like Kerima. Had the spider bitten her? Isn't that what some of them did? Paralyse you with their venom and then suck all the fluid out of your body. Beth knew her mouth was dry. And the thing seemed to be still — still enough to be concentrating on sucking the life from her. Its only movement was in its hair which rippled as if a gentle breeze were breathing through it. Kerima was getting further and further away. The only reality was Beth's hand, encased in spider.

But she must fight! Of course she had to fight! She glared down at the filthy spider. Not even a vacuum cleaner would sort this one out. This really was the creature of her worst nightmare. And that's just what this was! A nightmare. Not real.

This spider is not real, she told her mind. Over and over she repeated the words to herself. This spider does not exist. This spider is a figment of my imagination. This is not real and I refuse to see it. I will not see this spider anymore. I am holding Kerima's hand. This spider is simply Kerima's hand.

Sure enough, very gradually the spider began to blur and fade, and Kerima's long, smooth fingers were once again draped across Beth's palm. Beth's chest thumped and heaved. Cool, delicious, fragrant air pumped life back into her. She was winning! She... Granta's eye glowed dimly on Kerima's hand, and then vanished. *I'll be back!* growled a voice in her head. *I'll be back!*

I will not be afraid, she answered the voice. You will not destroy me. I am strong enough to fight your power. Hollow, menacing laughter filled her head, but she forced it back, shoving it away with her mind until her head was clear.

Beth looked at Kerima. Kerima seemed to be completely unaware of the drama that had just unfolded right beside her. She still gazed vacantly into nothingness. Beth let go of her hand and stood up.

It was only then that she realised just how much her battle with Granta had taken out of her. Her feet were numb. She looked down at them as if they belonged to someone else. She was trembling uncontrollably. But, she thought, I won! *This time*, said a little voice inside. But she shoved it away. I will not be a victim! Next stop, Daisy, she thought. If everyone's suffering from delusions maybe, just maybe, the eye is still wherever she hid it. At least, I must try and get some sense out of her.

Beth scrabbled on the floor under Daisy's desk. "When was the last time you hoovered under here? Urgh! There's a lump of...I don't want to think what it's a lump of!"

Daisy sat all scrunched up on the edge of her bed. "It isn't there, Beth. I promise. It's just disappeared."

Finally, Beth had to accept that the eye was not there. "Did you throw it away? You know, dump it?"

Daisy shook her head. "All I know is, it was there, and then it wasn't. And it still isn't."

"I think we have to work on the idea that someone has taken it. Who could have taken it? Did you tell anyone where it was? Could your mum or dad have found it?"

"Look, Beth, you've seen where it was. Can you actually imagine the parentals accidentally stumbling across it?"

Beth wiped her hands on her jeans again. "No, I guess not."

"I..." Daisy looked uncomfortable. "Oh, no, it doesn't matter."

"Yes! Yes it does matter! Everything matters.

Come on Daisy, what were you going to say?"

"I did show it to Ashleigh."

"Did she touch it?"

"No. I wouldn't let her."

"Well, could she have taken it without you knowing?"

"No. I was with her all the time — and she and Toby left five minutes after I'd shown it to her. No, it wasn't Ashleigh." Daisy spoke so firmly that Beth nearly believed her. She wanted to believe her. But if Ashleigh had not taken it, then who? "It's disappeared," said Daisy as if she heard Beth's silent question. "Granta's moved it."

Beth thought about that. Could Granta have hidden the eye from them to punish them? To make it impossible for them to replace the eye? It did not feel quite right.

"Granta is messing with our minds," Beth spoke slowly. "We have to accept that, however crazy it seems. But he has not made real things happen."

"I nearly drowned! That was real enough!"

"Yes, I know that, but he put thoughts in your head, to make you have to go to the water. He didn't just create a pool of water and put you in it. Don't you see the difference?"

"No," Daisy spoke sulkily. "Besides, how do we know just what Granta is capable of? How do we know that he can't magic the eye away? He can certainly magic himself into our heads!"

Beth sat beside Daisy on the bed. "You're

right," she said wearily. "So, what can we do?"

"What about that Mike Todd guy?"

"Who?"

"You know, the curator bloke — the one who wrote the article in the local rag."

"Right. What about him?"

"I don't know, maybe he knows more than he's saying. Maybe he can give some advice on how to combat the powers of the eye."

"He said the only way to save yourself from the eye was to return it to Granta." Beth studied Daisy, trying to work out what she was thinking.

"Oh, I don't know, then. I just thought maybe he was only saying that to scare whoever stole it — us — into getting the eye back to the museum."

"So, maybe he knows more than he's saying?"

"Maybe. I mean, perhaps there's another way of getting around this Instata curse?"

"Right! You're right. It's a small chance, but it's the only one we've got at the moment. Come with me, Daisy? Let's go see this Mike Todd. Come on Daisy, it's worth a try!"

"What are you going to say to him? 'Well, we stole the eye, but we've lost it, and now we need to know how to stop Granta's magic without returning the eye, because we haven't got it to return?' I can see the blue lights flashing already. You'll be locked up in a police cell, then transferred to a mental hospital, and Granta will have his evil way — whatever that might be!"

"Well, someone's got to try!" Beth knew she was shouting too loud. All the pent-up fear, anger and frustration seemed to explode out of her. "You just sitting here feeling sorry for yourself! Kerima away with the wretched fairies. Amy in some weird coma that the medical profession can't explain! We're desperate, you stupid, stupid girl!"

Daisy bowed her head as if that would make the words bounce away from her. Beth continued, "Perhaps I should just give up too. Be too frightened to try and do anything!"

"Please don't." Daisy's voice was barely audible. "Go and see Mike Todd, think of a way of getting some information from him without giving yourself away. But I can't help, Beth, I can't! Everytime I move, the water surges up in my head, I feel myself drowning again. It's all I can do to sit here and concentrate on keeping Granta at bay!"

Beth wanted to slap the meek little face with all her force. But what was the point? She strode to the door. "Yes, Daisy, I'll think of something."

"Ashleigh might help," whispered Daisy. Beth knew Daisy was doing her best. It was no use being furious at her. She had suggested going to see Mike Todd, she was trying to help. She was just too weak to do anything.

"Okay, Daisy. Maybe I'll ask her. Look, don't worry. It's going to be all right. I know it is. Remember it's only your imagination. Just like a story that you make up yourself. If you start to believe in Granta's images, you're lost. It's down to you — you can choose any ending you want — but you must believe in it."

On the pavement outside Daisy's house, Beth paused, as if trying to decide which way to go. The cold, grey drizzle seemed to seep right inside her, adding to the heavy, waterlogged feeling that already weighed her down.

At least she now knew that the battle was real. Her sightings of spiders had been explicable enough — until now. Daisy and Kerima refused to fight what was happening and seemed to have stabilised in a sort of state that their parents accepted as flu. Amy, who Beth was now convinced had fought hard against Granta, was in a coma. Beth knew she had a choice. Join Daisy and Kerima and sit and wait to see what happened next. Or...or what? End up like Amy? No, she told herself firmly, or take action!

She hesitated before knocking on the heavy wooden front door. But only for a moment. It was Ashleigh who answered the door.

"Beth! What can I do for you?"

"Can I come in?" Beth knew of Ashleigh's feelings towards Amy and she was not sure if she felt the same towards her.

"Yeah, of course! You look lousy!"

Beth smiled. "Thanks," she said. "Knowing that makes me feel really good!"

"Oh, I'm sorry, it's just..."

"Yeah, I know. Look," Beth glanced through

the hall into the kitchen where Ashleigh's mother was unpacking some shopping, "can we go to your room, or something?"

"I'm intrigued!" laughed Ashleigh. "Come on."

"Have you spoken to Daisy?" asked Beth as Ashleigh shut the bedroom door.

"Not since before the weekend. I was going to pop round there later. Isn't it great to have a week off school? Mind you, there's a load of homework to do."

"Yeah. Look, Ashleigh, there's trouble. I need your help."

Ashleigh eyed Beth suspiciously. "What kind of trouble? What has Amy been up to?"

"It's not Amy, well... Oh look, for heaven's sake, you know about the eye, because Daisy showed it to you. Amy's in hospital, Kerima's ill in bed with flu and ten stitches in her hand, and Daisy nearly drowned at the weekend, and is losing her grip on reality as we speak. I need your help!" Beth angrily swiped away the tears forming in her eyes.

Ashleigh was unmoved. "I don't see how I can help. I told Daisy what I thought. I told her to get rid of it. It was a crazy thing to do and..."

"Okay, okay!" Beth's voice was a low growl. "Message received and understood."

"Why don't you just put the thing back?"

"Well, either Daisy took your advice, or someone has nicked the thing." Beth glared hard at Ashleigh. "And whoever has taken that evil eye is in for a nasty shock."

"If you're trying to imply that I know anything about it…"

"I'm not *implying* anything! I just want you to understand that three people who've been in contact with the eye are ill — Amy in particular. And…" Beth was going to say that she was only hanging on by the skin of her teeth, that she did not know how much longer she could fight. But she did not want to hear the words said out loud. Somehow that would make her own collapse that much nearer. But she would not collapse, she could not! Not without a fight.

But she was running out of weapons. She just hoped that Mike Todd could give her some hope. Something to fight with.

It felt strange going into the museum. There were lots of adults with small children, forcing education down their throats during half-term, thought Beth. Beth made her way to what she thought of as Granta's Gallery. Would it still be there, or would they have removed it until the eye was returned?

The moment she entered the gallery, Beth knew the answer to her question. She knew even before she saw the small crowd of people peering round each other, and craning to read the caption beside the bizarre creature.

Beth hung back. Of course, all the publicity had drawn the crowds in. People were keen to see the keeper of human fears and to wonder at the audacity of the infamous thief. At last Granta stood alone, without anyone cluttering his view of the room.

Beth walked slowly towards the pride of the Instata. She stood, glaring at Granta, fixing his one good eye with her own determined stare. She could see the smooth curve of the empty eye socket. How easy it must have been for Amy to pop the eye out. Beth wished Granta's face would move. Respond to her presence. But nothing happened.

"Come on!" she whispered. "Prove your power to me." The purple eye stayed impassive.

Then Beth saw a change. The empty eye socket darkened. It seemed to come to life. No, it wasn't coming to life. There was something in it.

A long spindly leg eased its way out, then another, then another. Not hairy this time, more crab-like. Beth's mouth went dry and her heart quickened in spite of herself, but she was not afraid. She knew Granta was toying with her, this was a show of strength, not a real challenge. He would save that for when she was least expecting it.

Silence echoed in her ears. Then a vaguely familiar voice crashed through the silence, startling her.

"Hello!"

Beth spun round to face the speaker.

Chapter 9

"Sorry, I didn't mean to startle you. It's just that I recognised you. You were with that school party, the one that was here when the eye," Mike Todd nodded towards Granta, "was stolen." He smiled down at her.

He may remember me, thought Beth, but he looked like he'd forgotten to shave that morning.

"Oh, right! Hi!" Beth managed to smile. She cleared her throat, to give herself time to organise her thoughts. "I — it's half-term," she said lamely.

"Never!" Todd glanced around at the various children milling about the room, and shook his head. "I thought they were all playing hooky — I was just about to call the police."

She smiled. "What I meant was, we have to do a project. That's why I'm here. I decided to look at Granta and the Instata and their customs and powers." Beth tried to stretch her smile wider.

Todd looked her up and down. She shifted uncomfortably. "The police still haven't found the missing eye," he said. "They didn't manage to trace that guy your friend saw."

Beth knew she was blushing. "It's such a shame. I mean, plundering such a valuable item."

"Yeah," he shrugged. "I can't understand the mentality of people who do these things. Did the police give you a hard time?"

"No, not really. I think they knew we were telling the truth."

"Oh, well, if you do think of anything else, I hope you'll come forward, because..."

"Oh! I would, I would!" Beth nodded enthusiastically.

"Great. Ah well," he began to turn away. "Excuse me, it was good to see you."

"Mr Todd, please wait," said Beth. "I wondered if you'd help me. You know, with my project? I, er, read your article the other day and..." The curator stopped and turned back to her. He pushed dark brown hair out of his eyes which danced mischievously.

"My article?"

"Yes, Mr Todd." Beth began to feel extremely uncomfortable. Todd burst out laughing.

"Well, I hope you aren't going to base your essay on that! I was certainly interviewed by the local rag — and they did print edited highlights of that interview. They also embellished it with their own interpretation of disasters associated with the magic of the Instata."

Just for a moment, Beth felt relief flooding through her. It was all nonsense — all embellishments. But then she remembered the events of the past few days. They could not be dismissed as embellishments. Even so, she said, "So, you don't think that the person or people who took the eye are in any danger from Instata magic, then?"

He looked at her very carefully and Beth

kicked herself. She must watch what she said. Todd did not take his eyes off her as he spoke. "That's not what I said. I think that whoever took the eye is in grave danger. I believe..." He broke off and glanced at his watch. "Look," he said, "I've got half an hour or so. If you're genuinely interested in the Instata, why don't you come to my office and I'll answer your questions."

"Oh, thank you, Mr..."

"It's Mike," he said as he turned away. "Oh, by the way," he paused so that she could tell him her name, which she did, "Beth, you seem to have forgotten your notebook. I'll lend you one."

"I didn't expect...I just came to look..." Beth stuttered as she trotted along behind Mike. "I — thank you."

Mike Todd's desk was a mess. Stacks of paper, books, pencils, phone messages, note pads, bits of rock, stone, and bone, all jostled for position. The surrounding shelves sagged with papers and folders.

"Rule number one," said Mike, plunging his hand under a stack of paper, "be prepared!" He handed her a reporter's notebook.

She couldn't help laughing. "Thanks."

He saw her looking around his office. "There is method in my madness — I can assure you! Right, where do you want to start?"

Beth listened intently as Mike answered her questions. She found herself mesmerised by what he was saying. Fascinated by the customs and cultures of a tribe that had now vanished

112

from existence. She made notes and asked more questions. Mike began to wind the conversation up, and she realised that now was the time to ask the one question she needed an answer to. She must phrase it carefully.

"So you reckon whoever took the eye is in real danger?"

"Yes, yes I do," he nodded enthusiastically. He was totally relaxed, leaning back in his chair, stretching his legs out to the side of the desk. He was clearly talking about a subject he was confident about. "As I say, that newspaper took some of the more outlandish examples, and added a few frilly bits just to make them even more implausible. But my research shows that there are clear indications of genuine links between Instata magic and personal tragedies."

"That's amazing." Beth shook her head. "What if you accidentally interfered — like the cleaner that knocked over one of the icons?"

"Well, it's impossible to judge. I have my reservations about that story. But, at the same time, how can we possibly tell if the Instata's magic discriminates between wilful destruction and accidents?"

"It's frightening." Beth was distracted, thinking of the way Granta was interfering with her mind. Thinking of her three friends.

"Yes, it is. And in many ways it's a good thing that there are only a few remaining Instata relics in the world."

"I mean," Beth's palms were sweating. She

suddenly felt claustrophobic in the cluttered office. A new and petrifying thought had just struck her. "We don't know," she met Mike's eyes, aware that she must keep her gaze steady and untroubled, "what would happen if the eye was returned."

Mike looked puzzled, and raised an eyebrow.

"Well," she continued, battling to keep her voice steady, "if whoever took the eye does put it back, there's no reason to suppose that Granta's powers will leave them alone... They will still have interfered with..." Her stomach contracted fiercely at the thought she was struggling to express.

"No," said Mike matter-of-factly. "There's no guarantee that the danger from the protective powers surrounding Granta will miraculously evaporate — leave the thief alone — with the return of the eye. We simply don't know enough about this kind of power — many people, the majority in fact, choose to believe it's a load of nonsense. But then most people have no reason to fear it."

"Do you think it will be returned?" Beth managed to keep her eyes locked with his.

He shrugged. "I hope so, because I believe it's a beautiful artefact that should be enjoyed and admired. One of the few remaining clues to an amazing civilisation which has gone forever. I'm glad that whoever took it might be suffering right now. As far as I'm concerned this was a religious icon, and what the thief has done is tantamount to going and trashing a church nowadays." His posture was still languid, but she could see the muscles in his neck knotting as he spoke.

She must have looked troubled, because he suddenly beamed at her, rubbing his hand across his stubbled chin. "Hey, look, don't worry! Though why you should be worried about some thieving maniac, I don't know. There was a documented case, many years ago, where a thief looted an Instata Temple. The guy was either plagued by magical demons, or had a natural fit of remorse and replaced everything. According to records, he lived to the ripe old age of ninety-six! He was ninety-five when he committed the crime, but..."

Mike saw the look of horror on Beth's face. "That last bit was a joke, Beth. He was in his forties when he ransacked the Temple."

Beth laughed, hoping that it was convincing. So, the only thing that would give them a chance would be to return the eye. Her heart sank. She had so hoped that there might be a formula to defeat the magic woven over Granta. An ancient remedy left by the Instata to protect those who accidentally crossed swords with their extraordinary magic. But, if there was, it was obvious that Mike Todd was unaware of it. And he knew a heck of a lot about the Instata. Besides, Granta's eye had not exactly fallen into Amy's hands by accident.

Beth wondered for the hundredth time what

exactly had made Amy take the wretched thing in the first place. But there was no point wondering. She had to find a solution to the problem — not the root cause of it.

Perhaps she should tell Mike everything? He seemed so kind. Maybe he'd come up with a solution? After all, the situation was desperate — she so needed to talk to someone sympathetic.

"Mike..."

"Yes?"

An overwhelming surge of sadness filled her. She could not tell him. What was the point? His last story was comforting — to a degree. But she did not have the rotten eye to replace, did she? Besides, what would happen if she told him? The police would get involved — all hell would break loose. And he'd hate her. Somehow that mattered. It mattered a lot.

But what mattered most of all was the fact that there was no eye — and without it there really was no hope. She had at least to find the eye, before she went to anyone for help. But where to start?

"Hello, Beth —" Mike was leaning forwards over the chaotic desk, "the lights are on, but the house is empty!"

"Oh, sorry, nothing, I was just wondering what someone would do with the eye of Granta. That's all."

"Often you find plunderers are a bit like magpies. They take pretty things, just because they like to have them. You'll probably find that whoever has it, has a stash of gewgaws — bit like a kid's collection of marbles and conkers. Mind you, with this particular trinket, they may find more to it than meets the eye!" he paused, and when Beth didn't react, he continued. "Okay, bad joke! Now then, I really must get on."

"Yes, of course," Beth stood up. "Thanks so much for your time." Her only suspect was Ashleigh. She did not really strike Beth as the magpie type.

"Not at all," Mike was on his feet, offering her a warm, dry hand, "you've been a most attentive and searching audience — darn sight more rewarding than these monstrous school parties that get trooped in against their will!"

Beth felt the blood surge into her cheeks. "I — er..." How could she have thought he was dull?

His grin nearly split his face. "Anyway, Beth, let me see it when it's finished." He was ushering her out of his office.

"What?" She looked at him blankly.

"Your project — wasn't that..."

"Oh, yes, of course. Of course I will. Thanks again." She shot out of his office, and out of the museum as fast as she could without seeming rude. At the door she felt an urge to go and see Granta again. But she knew exactly what he looked like without having to stand in front of his all-seeing image. She knew that what she had to do was find his eye and give it back to him.

Images of spiders kept tumbling into her

mind. She did not know when Granta would make his next serious attempt on her mind. The sight of that grotesque spider in her hand whilst she sat with Kerima would be difficult to forget. His next trick was bound to be worse than that. She had to find the eye before that. She had to. Even though she knew the spiders were just images planted in her head by Granta, they were so real, so powerful. You could feel them, touch them. She did not know how long she could exercise the power of her mind over Granta's matter.

But, where to start? Where to go next? There did not seem to be any clues. Who on earth would have taken the eye from under Daisy's desk? Her mind kept coming back to Ashleigh. She really was the only outside link. But she was so convincing.

Beth kicked a stone on the pavement. Here she was, willing and eager to sort this whole mess out — but there was nothing she could do. She felt like she was in a maze with no exits. She felt like tearing all the bushes down — and stamping on them. She felt like screaming at the world and hammering at it with her fists.

She felt so alone.

She decided to visit Amy in the hospital. Maybe seeing Amy would give her inspiration.

She met Amy's dad at the swing doors as she entered the ward where Amy had a room on her own. She greeted him with expectant eyes. But his pale, haggard face and dull eyes told her all she needed to know. He started to speak to her, but his eyes filled up and his voice thickened.

She squeezed his arm, trying not to cry herself. "I'll just go sit with her for a while. Get yourself a coffee."

"You're a good friend, Beth." He tried to smile. Then he closed his eyes. "How much tragedy can hit one family?" He whispered. "First Ben, and now," he struggled to say her name, "now, Amy."

Beth could say nothing but she felt a new ring of responsibility wedge itself heavily over her shoulders.

Beth sat uncomfortably beside Amy. She didn't know whether to speak or to stay quiet. Amy looked so peaceful, it seemed almost criminal to disturb her by talking. But then she remembered the extremely violent unpeaceful way Amy had got into this state. How unwilling she was to be wherever she was.

"Amy," her voice sounded edgy. "Amy, it's Beth. I'm not going to lie to you. Things aren't brilliant. There's good news and there's bad news. You can't choose which you'd rather hear first, so I'll decide for you. The good news is, if we can return Granta's eye, we stand a chance of getting out of this mess. The bad news is, I still haven't found the wretched thing. And, at the moment, I can't think what to do next. Where to look next. But I will."

Beth paused. In a rush she realised how fond she was of Amy — how all the awful things that had happened over the last few weeks did not matter. They were friends. They would do anything for each other. Suddenly she couldn't stop speaking.

"Or, you never know, maybe a miracle will come along! Anyway, the main thing is that you hang on in there. You've got to get better, because I've managed to get you a job at The Coffee Stop — and you've always said you wanted a job, and..." Beth had not even realised she was crying until she felt her tears splashing onto her own hands. "You know I..."

She took a tissue from the box by Amy's bed and blew her nose hard. She heard the door creak open. It was Amy's dad.

"Beth, one of your school friends is outside — seems very anxious to speak to you."

"Okay. Look," she couldn't meet his eyes, "I'll come again very soon." But he was already engrossed in watching his pale, still daughter. Holding her hand and murmuring to her.

Beth retraced her steps along the hospital corridors. Why did they always smell like a mixture of disinfectant and school dinners? She wondered who she would find waiting for her. She couldn't help hoping it wouldn't be Daisy or Kerima. She didn't think she could cope with supporting either of them right now.

In fact, the figure that moved anxiously towards her when she came out of the main entrance of the hospital was the last person on earth she expected to see.

Chapter 10

Danny King looked extremely worried and uncomfortable.

"How's Amy?" he said. He had his collar turned up against the cold. His blonde hair stood up from his head, giving him a surprised look. His voice was gruff, almost aggressive.

"What's it to you?" Beth didn't know why she felt so belligerent towards him.

"I — I like — I — I was worried about her. I came to the hospital as soon as I heard. I didn't like to go in, so I've been hanging around outside. Then I saw you — I tried to catch you before you went in. I recognised Amy's father and I asked, and..."

"Yeah, okay, I get the picture." Beth could barely believe the usually cocky, self-assured Danny King was in such a state. Then it struck her that he was genuinely worried. More gently she said, "Why didn't you ask Amy's dad how she is?"

He grinned sheepishly. "I...look, stop being awkward and tell me how she is."

"Not good. She's in a sort of deep, deep sleep. She hasn't come round since she's been in there."

"What, a coma?"

"They're not calling it that." Beth started walking away from the hospital and Danny fell in beside her. "So," she said, glancing at him sideways, "does Kerima also have the benefit of your concern?"

His cheeks coloured up and she thought he was going to embark on another stutter. "She wouldn't speak to me," he said.

"Oh," said Beth, surprised that he had tried to speak to Kerima.

"Mind you, it was quite late when I phoned. It's desperate trying to get a bit of privacy in my house. It's not just my mother and father, it's my sister and my little brother — he's a right snoop. Always listening in on my conversations, always interfering. Have you got brothers and sisters?"

"No," said Beth. But she was no longer with Danny. Her mind was racing at his words. She knew something had been nagging at her, and Danny King had inadvertently given her the clue to what it was. It wasn't much, but it was something to follow up. She had to go and see Daisy again. Now.

She realised that she had speeded up her pace considerably and that Danny was matching her step for step. "I'd leave Kerima alone for a while if I were you," she said.

He nodded. "I know, I hurt her, but..." He stopped walking and Beth had to stop too. "Look, Beth, do you think Amy's dad...or Amy, would mind if I visited her?"

She looked at Danny as if for the first time. He really cared about Amy, she thought. It wasn't just guilt. He liked Amy. "I think they'd both be delighted," she said.

"Right!" he said. "Well, I'll see you back at school — or maybe at the hospital." He walked back towards the hospital. Beth shook her head and smiled to herself. Who'd have thought Danny King had a heart? Who'd have thought it would be Amy to find it? Well, well, well! She enjoyed the revelation for a full thirty seconds.

Then she thought that Amy might never know. Grimly, she headed for Daisy's house.

An hour later she left Daisy, a new destination on her mind. A glimmer of hope lightened her step. She took the cut through the park, skirting the lake. She saw a group of young kids coming towards her — three or four eleven year-olds. She moved off the path to let them past. One of them stuck her foot out, and Beth was not quick enough to leap it. She resigned herself to muddy knees and hands.

But she didn't hit the grass — she didn't stop falling. There was no ground to break her fall, she just kept tumbling into blackness. She kept expecting the ground to come up and meet her, but nothing. She was not spinning in a tunnel, there were no walls, just darkness, going on and on. She couldn't turn her head. She couldn't break her fall with her hands as she had intended — there was no ground to put them down on.

At last she thumped down hard onto soft, cold earth. At least, that's what she thought it was. The heels of her hands skidded on the soil and her cheek slapped down into a gooey mess.

She rolled onto her side and looked up expecting to see the group of kids standing over her laughing, or running off into the distance.

There was nothing, only darkness. She listened hard. A muffled, rushing sound like blood surging around her own body was all she could hear. Then something started falling on top of her. It was earth. Suddenly she knew what was happening. She was sloshing around in the bottom of a deep, deep hole. She was being buried alive! She tried to pull herself to her feet, but the sludgy mud held her down on her hands and knees. She tasted mud.

Then someone turned the lights on. And it wasn't mud at all. Crawling all over her body were spiders! Tiny ones creeping under her clothes, their legs fumbling for a hold on her flesh. She could feel them tickling and prickling against her skin. She put her hand to her face and scraped the sticky lump off. It was the huge spider of before — oozing thick, stinking green fluid through her fingers. Screaming she wiped at her cheek and tried to flick the thing off her hand. She was yelling, shaking, twisting and turning, trying to free herself of the clinging spiders.

The stink of the liquid weeping from their bodies made her gag and still the huge spider clung to her hand, its glassy eyes seeming to wobble as she shook at it. In fact, the grip of its eight hairy legs grew tighter and tighter, digging in to her hand, as if it had claws, and still the other spiders crawled all over her body, her face, her hair. She writhed around trying to get them off, trying to squash the spiders that swarmed all over her.

Her heart was beating so hard, she felt it would burst right through her ribs. The pain inside her was so great, she did not know what to do. Suddenly it was the pain that was controlling her, not the spiders. She was breathing too fast. Panting. Sucking air in and blowing it out. Suck, blow. Suck, blow. She must slow things down. She was going to faint. Worse, she was going to...

"Beth..." A voice swam through the pain. She knew it was a life raft. She had to cling to it. It was her only hope. Then she realised this was Granta. It was Granta's doing, of course! "Beth!" The voice called again, getting clearer and stronger now.

Not real, she said to herself. Not real.

"Come on Beth, fight it." The voice called again.

Light, real light began to filter into her vision. Trees and sky swam into sight. Ashleigh was leaning over her, shaking her. Ashleigh!

"I was coming to see you!" croaked Beth. "Then..." She caught sight of the group of eleven year-olds clustering around her and groaned.

"Get out of here!" yelled Ashleigh, lurching towards them menacingly. The kids scarpered.

"I — " Beth groaned again. She managed to sit up. Her eyes met Ashleigh's.

"Toby!" they both said together.

"We don't have much time," gasped Beth. "I can't take many more onslaughts like that one." She glanced down at herself. She was completely encased in mud. It had oozed into her coat, her shirt, her boots. "We have to get the eye. Have you got it? Where did Toby put it?"

"I don't know for sure that he has it," Ashleigh said. "It's just a feeling. He's gone sort of fluey, like the others. But it's not flu. I don't think he's hallucinating, but he obviously feels lousy — and it's like he's frightened. He's acting like a real baby."

"Oh, Ashleigh, if I'm like this, how are the others? We really have no time to lose. We've got to see if Toby took it."

"Calm down, Beth. Let's sit on this bench for a moment. Come on! You've had a shock."

Beth let herself be led to the bench. She tried to speak but Ashleigh wouldn't let her. "Listen to me, Beth. I went to visit the others — Daisy and Kerima — looking for you. They're still woozy, but they're stable. They're both lucid. I think Granta must be happy to hold them where they are. It's like he's mustering his full strength to unleash on you. You're the challenge, the one that's still going. The others have submitted. But you haven't, and you mustn't!" She took Beth's hand, and seeing blood beading through the mud, said, "Ouch! You must have landed in a bramble bush! I'll help you. Granta can't touch me. With me supporting you, we can sort this out."

Beth nodded. She glanced at her hand. There were scratches all over it. "It was so real, Ashleigh. I saw — " her mouth worked.

"It's okay, only tell me if you want to."

"No. Somehow if I say it, it makes it more real. Let's try and get the truth from Toby. I'm okay now," Beth gave a wobbly smile, "well, as okay as I'll be until we get that blessed eye back into its socket!"

Toby was in a sorry state. He looked at them with big, dark eyes. He had pulled the bed covers up to his chin.

"How are you?" Beth spoke in a gentle voice that at any other time would have sent Toby into a *don't-talk-down-to-me* riot of yelling. This time, however, he lapped up the soft sympathy and started to reply in a mumbly, whiny voice.

Ashleigh's stern voice made both him and Beth jump.

"Look, let's cut the nonsense. We think you've got the eye, Toby, so where is it?"

He looked blankly at them, and for a moment Beth experienced a surge of terror. What if Toby didn't have it? Then what? She did not know how much longer she would be in a fit state to think — let alone rush around trying to find the missing eye.

Toby started whimpering. "I don't like the dark!"

"I know you don't Toby. But it isn't dark now. Look out of the window, it's daytime." Toby looked and nodded.

"I'm cold," he said.

It didn't take much for Ashleigh to get exasperated with her brother and she was fast reaching major irritation levels. "You're ill Toby, that's why you're cold. You have flu!"

Toby looked as if he were about to cry. Beth touched Ashleigh's hand and indicated to Ashleigh to be quiet for a moment. Ashleigh shrugged and glared at Toby. The three of them sat in silence for a good five minutes. At last Beth spoke; she could not be sure, but she thought Toby had been trying to help. He was just too poorly and scared to string his thoughts together.

"Is the eye somewhere cold and dark, Toby?"

"What, like the fridge?" snorted Ashleigh. Beth glared at her. Fortunately Toby was concentrating on Beth. His eyes widened and he looked startled by her words. He seemed to see Beth in a new light. Beth realised that as much as anything he was weighing up just how much trouble he was going to get into.

"Toby, we're not angry. You won't be punished," she said. He glanced at his sister and Ashleigh attempted to make her nod sincere. "We'll all have problems if we don't return the eye, though."

"Who?" he demanded, regaining some energy at the prospect of not getting into too much trouble. "If I did have that eye, which I'm not saying I do, why should I tell you where it is? You're always nasty to me, calling me names, leaving me out. I should tell the police and then..."

Beth thought Ashleigh would hit him. Beth herself felt like throttling the little creep. Thank heavens she didn't have any brothers or sisters!

"Look, Toby, we are in a serious mess, the police are involved, and yes, you could go and tell them about all this. But where does that leave you? Do you know what questions they'll ask?" Beth managed to stay calm, but it was getting harder for her to think straight. The forces of Granta's evil cloyed to her mind, making it feel like over-cooked scrambled eggs. "They'll ask why you didn't talk to them sooner. They'll wonder how come you have the eye, they'll..."

"Oh for heaven's sake, Beth, save the child psychology for a more worthy cause. Listen Tobe, you know that video game you've been wittering on about? We'll get it for you, okay? Now come on, where's the eye?"

"When?" Both girls looked at him blankly. "When will I get the video game?"

"Tomorrow!" said Beth. "You can have it tomorrow."

Toby shivered. It was almost as if he could not quite bring himself to tell them. "I, I feel very strange — sort of frightened. Sort of dark and cold..." he said at last.

"It's your flu," said Beth. "The eye is strange and it can give you flu, and if you want to get better, and get the video game, you must tell us where you put the eye."

"It's in the cellar," his eyes darkened slightly and he shuddered as if at the memory.

"The cellar!" said Ashleigh. "But you hate it down there — besides, you're not allowed..."

"Great," said Beth. "Thanks, Toby! Your present will come! But," and she paused threateningly, "if you breathe a word about any of this to anyone — ever — terrible things will happen to you. The eye is evil!" Toby turned his head away. Beth pulled a face at Ashleigh. "Come on, if we're quick we can still make the museum."

Ashleigh glanced at her watch. "Okay! Oh, Toby, whereabouts in the cellar did you put it?"

"It's dark down there. There were all bottles and boxes and damp patches. And it was cold."

"Good grief! Stop being a baby! Where did you put it?"

"In Dad's wine."

"Excellent!"

But it was not excellent.

EVIL EYE

Chapter 11

Armed with torches, the girls made their way down the tight, dark stairs into the musty-smelling cellar. Toby was right, there was a jungle of boxes, and bits of old furniture, and off-cut chunks of carpet — and cobwebs. Beth turned her mind off —. besides, real spiders were the least of her worries.

The main problem was that Ashleigh's and Toby's dad had a wicked collection of wine. Lots of it was stacked in wooden wine racks, some of it was still in cardboard boxes or crates. But there was gallons of the stuff. Where to start?

They tried Toby again, but got nowhere fast. It soon became clear that in his anxiety to get out of the cellar, he'd simply dumped the eye. If they were lucky it would have ended up somewhere in the wine collection.

In the end, Ashleigh took the boxes and crates, and Beth took the racks.

"Whatever you do, don't touch it! Even if it's still in that little jewellery box, I wouldn't trust it. At least with those boxes you stand a chance of seeing it first," said Beth, as she started pulling dusty bottles out of the rack and groping around in the hole created with an unseeing hand.

Nearly an hour later the girls were exhausted, grubby and disillusioned. What if they searched every inch of the cellar and still didn't find it? But then, at last, Beth pulled a bottle of wine from the rack and a small box fell out.

"Ashleigh!" Ashleigh walked over. "I've found it!" Beth felt tears of relief in her eyes. Her insides flipped, and the tension and aching of her limbs and body seemed to evaporate. "I've found it," she whispered, and opened the box. There it was. Granta's eye.

Ashleigh beamed torch light on to it. Beth was determined not to look at the eye, but its force demanded her attention. It gleamed darkly up at her, seeming to soak up the light from the torch.

She felt herself being drawn into the eye. Such power, she thought.

"Put the lid on and let's get out of here, before my mum and dad realise what's gone on. As it is, when Dad comes to get a bottle of wine, he'll be out for blood!"

"I'm so glad you're here, Ashleigh," said Beth, placing the lid firmly on the box. "I'm feeling really awful again."

The girls clambered up to the house.

"We've missed the museum," said Ashleigh. "Can you last another night?"

"I'll have to," said Beth. "Besides, just knowing we have the eye to put back, is such a relief."

"Why don't you stay here the night?"

"Thanks Ashleigh. I don't want to be alone. I'm not sure what would happen. It's beginning to feel almost like I should give myself to Granta. Add myself to his collection of fears. I'll phone Mum."

"Don't even think it Beth! You mustn't. If you find yourself thinking like that, you must say to yourself 'I am Beth, I will not give myself to you, I am Beth, leave me alone,' or something like that."

Beth nodded. "I just feel so tired." Beth looked at Ashleigh with big eyes. "I feel as if I could sleep forever."

Ashleigh put her arms around Beth and they hugged. Neither of them could speak.

Beth was too frightened to sleep — and Ashleigh was too worried to let her sleep. So, the two girls talked and read all night. At last the first grimy smears of wintry dawn began to appear across the sky. The girls began to relax.

The next time Ashleigh looked out of the window not a trace of night was left. She realised with horror that she had fallen asleep. She looked over to where Beth lay in a sleeping bag, on a mattress on the floor. Beth's head lolled off the pillow and onto the floor, her mouth was slack. There was no visible sign of breathing.

Ashleigh hurled herself on to the floor and began shaking Beth.

"Beth! Oh, Beth!"

Beth's eyes shot open. "Ashleigh!"

"Come on, Beth, fight it!" said Ashleigh.

"Cool it, Ashleigh, I'm all right! Mind you,

being woken up like that is enough to send a girl out of her mind!" Beth said groggily, rubbing her eyes. She grinned at Ashleigh. "I'm okay. I must have fallen asleep — into such a deep sleep that even old Granta couldn't penetrate it!"

"Thank goodness. All I can say is that you should always sleep with the lights off! Now, what time is it? Seven thirty — the museum opens at ten, yes?"

Beth nodded. Her head felt congested. She thought of the eye under her pillow — she hadn't wanted Ashleigh to be anywhere near it. What if putting it back did not work? She remembered Mike Todd's story of the guy who ransacked the temple — and then returned his booty. She had to believe that story was true. She had to.

At nine thirty they were ready to leave. Beth's stomach churned with a mixture of excitement and fear. A cocktail that threatened to have her rushing to the loo every five minutes. But she knew she would be better once they were on their way. And, with the eye safely tucked in Beth's pocket, the two girls headed for the museum.

It was not there.

Beth and Ashleigh stood in the mystic gallery filled with disbelief. Granta was gone.

Before either of them could put their shock into words, Beth spotted Mike Todd in the corridor. Grabbing Ashleigh's arm, she dashed towards his disappearing back.

"Mike!"

He turned. "Beth? What is it? You look frantic. Something you missed for your project?"

"Granta's gone!"

He smiled ruefully. "Yep, and I can't say I'm sad to see the back of him. I only wish we could have returned him all in one piece."

"Returned?" demanded Beth. Mike looked puzzled.

"Granta and the other Instata artefacts were part of a travelling exhibition." He glanced at his watch. "They're headed back to a London gallery — in fact, I'd say they're being loaded onto a train right now."

Beth could not speak. She felt her face begin to wobble, her eyes begin to fill. Ashleigh took her arm. "Come on Beth, it's time we left."

Beth shook her arm free. "No!" she said. She looked Mike Todd hard in the eyes. He was beginning to look extremely concerned at this strange behaviour. In a low, hard voice she said, "I have the eye in my pocket. We need to get it back into Granta's head before any more damage is done. One person is in hospital, and four others are on their way there. You have to help us."

If there had been a chair, Mike Todd would have thumped down into it. Instead he leant against the wall.

"You!" he said. "You." The look of complete disgust in his eyes was not lost on Beth.

"Yes," she said wearily. She couldn't fight him too. Besides there was no time to explain. "Me. Now, are you going to help or not? You can take us to the police — but you only risk more people touching it. And that, I can tell you, is a frightening prospect. That statue should carry a government health warning."

"We'll take my car," he said. "Come on."

He drove like a maniac. But Ashleigh was not in the mood for cracking driving jokes, and Beth was feeling increasingly distant from real life. She felt herself being beckoned into a darkness that was at once frightening and welcoming. She knew that if she entered it there would be no coming back. Somehow the prospect seemed quite appealing.

But Ashleigh kept muttering to her about her mum and dad, about the fact that they were driving past school, about getting her library books back, about hanging on in there.

"Leave me alone!" she heard herself moan. "Be quiet."

Mike Todd turned round and hissed at her, "Don't you dare give in! You'll put that eye back if it's the last thing you do! Do you hear me!"

Beth saw a girl who looked just like her. She was laughing — a raucous, grating laugh. It couldn't be her, could it? After all, she was here, wasn't she? But where was here?

The man who was driving turned to the girl

who looked like her again, and yelled. "Get back here, Beth!" His voice was not anxious or friendly, it was downright furious. She knew that she had to get back to him, if only to have the opportunity to explain the truth of what had happened.

The car had stopped and Mike and Ashleigh were staring at her. Her chest heaved and her breath was coming in great gasps. "It's okay," she managed to gasp, "I'm here. Let's find the..."

The three of them ran towards the station. The London train was in. It was delayed by five minutes. They had a chance.

They quickly found the freight carriage. A security guard lounged around — obviously employed because of the valuable cargo.

Mike spoke directly to Ashleigh for the first time. "I don't care what you do but distract that guard, get him out of there." He pulled a cap from his pocket. "Wear this, think of it as a disguise!" He grabbed Beth by the arm, digging his fingers hard into her muscle, holding on to her, and supporting her at the same time.

Thirty seconds later, Ashleigh and the guard came rushing off the train and hared down the platform.

Mike propelled Beth into the train. It wasn't difficult to locate the museum section, and Mike knew which package Granta was in. As carefully as possible, he removed the packaging. There was Granta's head, the empty socket looking like a dark scar in its distorted face.

Beth stood, transfixed.

"Don't just stand there, get the eye. The eye, Beth!"

With fumbling fingers Beth rifled through her pocket. She pulled out the little box that held the eye that had caused her and her friends so much pain. Her hand trembled as she inserted it back in the eye socket. The socket almost sucked it out of her fingers.

Nothing happened when the eye gleamed back in its rightful place, next to its twin. Nothing. Beth expected to be flooded with relief, but no, she was too drained to feel anything.

She was aware of Mike Todd on his hands and knees, fumbling with the packaging, trying to make it look exactly as it had been. She could hear a furore, raised voices, coming closer. Still she could not move. At last Mike Todd turned and pushed her from the train. Behind her she heard a gruff voice saying, "If I ever catch that little tyke I'll skin her alive!"

On the platform, Mike Todd turned to her and said, "I think you better make your own way..."

She did not hear the rest of the sentence, because everything went black.

She wasn't falling, she was being sucked along a long whirling passage. Images screamed past her. Images of death and contorted bodies. Spiders scrambled for a hold on her as she was dragged past, pulling at her face, her clothes, her hair. But as they touched her, their legs withered back into dead bodies.

There was Toby! He was slumped at the bottom of some steep stairs, in a dark, gloomy place. His head at an odd angle, his mouth gaping, his sightless eyes wide open. Suddenly light flooded across him, warming him, reforming him. He was getting to his feet.

Suddenly, Amy appeared, flames leaping from her. Now acrid, black smoke rose from her charred body. Her mouth looked like a hole in a piece of burnt paper. Then, like a film going backwards, Amy's flesh reappeared, growing onto her bones, firm and alive.

Amy was gone, and it was Kerima, drenched in blood, who now faced Beth. Her flesh was ripped all over and blood spurted from the gashes, spattering Beth. But, as Kerima disappeared behind her, Beth could see the blood being drawn back into the body and the wounds healing.

Now, water washed the blood from Beth's face and hands. Daisy's bloated, discoloured body suddenly bobbed up against her. Beth was incapable of screaming. Daisy's face looked like someone had pumped it up with a bicycle pump. But, miraculously, Daisy began to shrink to her normal size, and colour seeped into her face, she stood up and walked from the lake.

A jolt like an electric shock rocked Amy's body. She jerked bolt upright in her hospital bed, her eyes wide open, vague images fluttering in her mind. But there was Dad, sitting by her bedside.

"Amy? Amy!"

"Dad! Oh, Dad, I'm so sorry, I'm so sorry!"

"Sorry, Amy, you mustn't be sorry! You've come back to me!" Her dad was hugging her but Amy's head was full of one thought and one thought only. It was like she had been asleep until she could at last blurt out the truth.

"You don't understand," she sobbed. "I knew where Ben was that night! I knew he was at that warehouse. If I'd have told Auntie Claire, he'd still be alive. She actually asked me if I knew where he was and I didn't tell her. They would have gone and got him. He should be alive today. I killed him."

"Shh, shhh. Has this been worrying you all this time? Even if you'd said something, who knows? Oh, my love, it's not your fault. It's no one's fault, except for the morons who hold these parties in unsafe premises. You didn't know there'd be a fire! How could you blame yourself! Claire said you should have counselling, but I wouldn't hear of it. I don't like all those mind doctors and I wouldn't even consider it." Tears streamed down his face to mingle with Amy's. "Well, we're both going to get help. We are, we are."

Amy sobbed into his shoulder. She was here, she was alive. And at last she had told someone her dreadful secret.

The girls sat round in Kerima's snug room. Kerima was lounging on the floor, reading, with a neatly healing scar on her hand. Amy was playing patience. Daisy just slouched on the sofa, staring into space, and Beth sat at Kerima's desk, writing. She paused every now and then to suck on the end of her pen.

"Oh rats!" said Amy. "There's a card missing. I never feel as if I've won unless I complete each run!"

"Nine of spades," murmured Kerima.

"You knew! And you didn't tell me? I don't believe you!"

"It's so unlike you to do anything so dull as play patience, I thought it might add a bit of excitement to the game!" Kerima laughed.

All the girls smiled.

Amy pushed the cards away. "Yeah, well, seriously, I just want to thank you guys for everything, you know. We haven't really spoken about it much, and I'm learning it's best to talk about things."

"Heaven forbid!" said Daisy. "You'll not be talking more?"

Amy grinned. "Fair dos, but honestly... Thanks — particularly to you, Beth." The other two nodded their agreement.

Kerima looked back down at her book. "I spoke to Danny King this morning." No one could think of anything to say to this piece of information. "We're cool," she added.

Amy blushed. "Thanks Kerima. We're just friends — you know — me and DK."

"So he'll visit me on my sick bed then, will he?" asked Daisy smirking.

"I feel a subject change coming on!" said Amy.

"Agreed." Kerima smiled. "It's a shame Ashleigh's not here."

"She's coming later," Beth paused as she licked the flap of a large brown envelope. "Anyway guys, I must scoot! Got to post a letter — then work, you know how it is."

Beth met Ashleigh on the street outside Kerima's house.

"Beth! How are you?"

"Oh, not bad. Still a bit wobbly — but, then, I think we all are. I don't think any of us will be the same again."

Ashleigh nodded, her face serious. "No, none of us. Did you send the letter?"

Beth patted the envelope. "Now's the time. It's got the project in and just a note. You know, no finger pointing, just apologising. I don't know why it matters so much. I mean, Mike Todd isn't important, it's just..."

"I'm sure Mr Todd'll understand — probably even forgive, in time. Besides, that project is going to knock him dead — he'll probably hire you as a research assistant! Honestly, Beth, when you were out of it that last time he was so concerned, so kind." Ashleigh squeezed Beth's arm.

"He spent his whole time shouting at me on

the way to the station!" Beth knew that if Mike hadn't done that, she probably would have succumbed to Granta, but that wasn't the point. "And then, when I came round — just to dump us like that — and the things he said!"

"He didn't know the full story!"

"Well, he never will, will he?" demanded Beth. Ashleigh gave a non-committal shrug. But Beth did not really need an answer, she was in her own thoughts. "It doesn't really matter what he thinks or does. I just want to be allowed back in the museum again. I really like that place. Of course, it would be nice to put Mr Todd straight on a few things, but..." Beth clicked her tongue.

Ashleigh wondered whether to tell her that she had managed to speak to Mike Todd and tell him the full story of what had happened. She decided not to. Anyway, Beth was still rabbiting on.

"By the way, you never told me what you said to that guard on the train!"

"I said my dad was going mad in the end carriage and that everyone was screaming and he had to come quickly."

"An inspired story if I may say so! Thank goodness he was a brave guard, I bet some would have run a mile!"

"Oh, he didn't go to the carriage, he went and got a policewoman! When they arrived at the carriage, of course, everything was peaceful. But I was well out of sight by then.

When he turned round to grab me, and I'd vanished, his eyes must have popped out of his head!"

Beth groaned. "P-lease! Well, I better go post this." Beth smiled at Ashleigh.

"Yeah, okay then."

But the girls did not move. Then, as if reading each others' minds, they stepped together and, without a word, gave each other a quick hug before going their separate ways.